HEXING wITH A CHANCE OF TORNADOES:

A Paranormal Women's Fiction Romance Novel

MANDY M. ROTH

Published by Raven Happy Hour, LLC

Oxford, MS 38655

www.ravenhappyhour.com

Dedication

To every woman. Thank you for being you.

Grimm Cove Series

Cloudy with a Chance of Witchcraft

Hexing with a Chance of Tornadoes

Spellcasting with a Chance of Spirits

Blurb

A storm is brewing and so is a budding romance.

I've been told I'm a force to be reckoned with. That I blow onto the scene like a tornado. I've stopped caring if that's a compliment or a dig. Now I just wear it like a badge of honor. So when life threw me a curveball and I ended up going from a cushy job in New York City to the tiny Southern town of Grimm Cove, I thought I was ready for anything.

Ha! Not quite.

You see, Grimm Cove is teeming with supernaturals. And since I've known they exist for a hot minute, I'm still in a state of total shock. When I learn that I come from a long line of witches and demon slayers, the stakes (pun intended) get even higher and sharper.

These monsters aren't make-believe. They're out for blood.

I'm trying to decide if having the alpha of the local wolf-shifter pack nipping at my heels is an asset in this fight, or if he's one more person I need to watch my back around. I just wish he wasn't so sexy and didn't smell so good. He'd be a lot easier to resist. I have enough going on in my life as it is. I really do not have time for all this fated mate crap everyone keeps telling me about. My head and heart are at war and now isn't the time for distractions, especially since it's painfully clear that something evil wants me dead.

ONE

Jeffrey

JEFFREY FARKAS FINISHED POURING a beer for one of his regulars, Gilbert Carol.

The bar, Wolf's Moon Bar and Grill, was Jeffrey's pride and joy. He owned and operated it. The place catered to a lot of shifters like Gilbert, which was no real surprise, seeing as how Jeffrey was a wolf-shifter himself.

Like attracted like.

That had always been the way of it when it came to supernaturals and always would be. It was comforting being around others who were like him. And there was something to be said for safety in numbers. Besides, other species had their own hangouts around town, and while they did get the occasional straggler, nearly all were welcome.

There were exceptions to that, as noted by the table full of slayers drinking up near the entrance of the bar. They were only there to start shit, and everyone knew it.

Two nights back, one of the younger wolf-pack males had gotten himself into a spot of trouble a town over. He'd tied on a few too many and ended up in a fight outside a bowling alley. The man he'd traded blows with happened to be a slayer, and he hadn't taken kindly to getting his backside handed to him.

Jeffrey, on the other hand, found great amusement in it all. But he knew the second he'd gotten the call about it the slayers would be an issue. They weren't exactly known for being the forgive-and-forget kind.

And here they were, making themselves known in his place of business. It wasn't as if the town didn't have plenty of other watering holes for them to choose from. Ones they'd be welcomed at, rather than stick out like sore thumbs. Hell, the slayers even had their own bar. One that catered to their kind and was run by a retired slayer, or hunter, depending on who you asked for clarification of their job description or life calling.

They weren't at Jeffrey's establishment to drink

and relax. They were there to make a point and provoke an altercation.

Sitting in Wolf's Moon Bar and Grill was the equivalent to them throwing down the gauntlet and issuing a direct challenge to Jeffrey—the pack alpha. Wasn't the first time their leader, Elis Van Helsing, and he had gone head to head. And it wouldn't be the last.

The two had a long-standing history of pissing off one another to the point fights broke out. It was sort of their thing. And it was why they often found themselves seated before the Council of Elders, getting a verbal lashing and being put on the supernatural version of probation.

By this point, Jeffrey had lost count of the number of times he'd had to go before the council because of run-ins with Elis and his people.

Worth it.

He'd gladly accept any punishment the Elders wanted to hand out if it meant he could go a few rounds with Elis or his bestie, Kellan Harker. Both were assholes extraordinaire. Where one went, the other was sure to follow.

It was a case of the asshole leading the asshole.

Such was the case now.

There was something about Kellan, in particular, that bothered Jeffrey. Part of it was how much the guy smelled like a wolf. That could be easily explained if he had dogs for pets. But still, there was something about him that always left Jeffrey's wolf restless. It was as if his wolf was expecting to be challenged.

That was absurd. Kellan couldn't challenge him for pack leader because the man wasn't a shifter. He'd come onto the scene right before high school graduation and had been a thorn in Jeffrey's side ever since.

Kellan currently sat next to Elis in a show of solidarity. He was tapping on the table while his leg shook, as if he had nervous energy he needed to burn.

As Jeffrey stared over at them, Kellan lifted his bottle of beer and his middle finger. He then grinned before taking a swig.

Jeffrey's wolf stirred within him, wanting to be allowed out to play a fun game of eat-the-asshole-slayer and his equally assholey buddy.

He tempered the wolf down. It took some inner coaxing, but it finally paid off. The urge to shift forms and eat the men subsided, at least for now.

If Maria, the head of the Council of Elders, could see him now. She might just be proud of him. She was always harping on how he had to hold himself to a higher standard. He had to set an example. It was up to him to follow the very rules he was expected to enforce.

Blah, blah, suck-all-the-fun-out-of-the-room talk if you asked him.

But he got her drift.

Grimm Cove was a different kind of town. It was one where supernaturals and anything non-human seemed to congregate. Jeffrey wasn't sure of the hows or whys. It had simply always been that way. And while supernaturals were everywhere, Grimm Cove seemed to have an abnormally high ratio of them.

When Jeffrey had been in the military, he'd seen the world, going to places he'd never dreamed of going. While a number of the locations were spots that he never again wanted to have to visit, some had been nice. They'd even had groupings of supernaturals. But none had been like home.

Like Grimm Cove.

He'd been born and raised in the South Carolina town. His father had been the local wolf-pack alpha, and when he'd stepped down, that title and responsibility had passed to Jeffrey. The men in his family had an age-old tradition of doing what was expected of them.

As pack alpha, Jeffrey was the man in charge, at least in matters concerning wolf-shifters. They far outnumbered the other kinds of shifters in the area. His pack was the largest in the state, which was a source of pride for them. Jeffrey was the alpha in the state the others turned to when something major came up that needed to be handled, or when crap hit the fan.

It also meant he had to deal with assholes like the slayers.

"Order up," said Robbie Helens, the bar's current short-order cook, keeping Jeffrey from spiraling more over the slayers in his bar.

Robbie's brother Ryan picked then to enter the bar, and he gave a small wave in the direction of Robbie. Ryan's hair was wet, and he smelled heavy of soap, even from a distance, indicating he'd just showered and come straight over to the bar.

Stella, one of the bar's waitresses, headed for the kitchen pass-through window just as Robbie rang the small bell on the metal counter. She groaned. "You totally saw me coming already."

Robbie peered through the pass-through, grinning. "I did. But I know the bell annoys you." He then proceeded to ding the bell several more times, laughing as he did.

Stella grunted as she loaded the order of burgers and fries onto a serving tray. "One of these days I'm gonna shove that bell where the sun don't shine."

"Looking forward to it," teased Robbie. "But when you're done, can I shove something up your—"

"Hey now," warned Jeffrey.

Stella lifted a hand. "I've got this."

Ryan chuckled as he took a seat at the bar. "Careful, brother, she's likely to take a chunk out of your hide."

True story, considering Stella was also a wolf-shifter. She was capable of doing a partial shift and it just so happened she could do so with her hands. Never fun to have a woman coming at you with dagger-sharp nails.

"Damn straight," she added and then growled lightly.

"Carry on," said Jeffrey, knowing better than to get in her path when she was in a mood.

"Got a feeling she'd be worth the trouble," added Robbie loudly from the kitchen. "So, about me shoving something up your backside?"

The look she shot Robbie was one that threatened vital parts of his anatomy without saying a word.

He put his hands up. "What? Honest question."

"Get your mind out of the gutter, Robbie," she said, this time smiling. "And if you're a good enough boy, maybe."

Jeffrey just shook his head at their antics. It was like he was privy to some bizarre mating ritual. One minute he was worried Stella might throw a beer bottle at Robbie and the next he was concerned he might have to usher everyone out of the bar to give the pair alone time.

Such had been the way of it since Robbie had been hired on as a cook. Jeffrey would be stunned if they weren't a hot item by the end of spring. The sexual tension between them was thick enough to choke on. There was a pool going on when they'd finally do the deed.

Jeffrey had a few bucks tied up in it all.

"What month did you pick for them to finally do the horizontal bop?" asked Gilbert, who was camped at the end of the bar on "his" stool. For his birthday the year prior, Jeffrey and some of his close friends had gotten Gilbert a shiny gold nameplate for it and everything. He lifted his beer, glancing in Stella's direction as she carried the tray of food to the table up near the front.

Jeffrey snorted and set about pouring Ryan a beer, already knowing what the man wanted. "Next month. You?"

"This one," said Gilbert.

Ryan guffawed and took his beer. "Gilbert might win."

"Maybe," added Jeffrey with an incline of his head.

Gilbert's gaze met his. "You know, people are taking bets on when you'll finally decide to hang your hat on a permanent hook."

Jeffrey lifted a brow. "Meaning when I'll get married because the odds of me finding my mate at my age are slim to none?"

Shifters, like some other species of supernaturals, were said to have a perfect match—a mate—someone who was the other half of their heart and soul.

At least that was what he'd been told. Sure, he knew his parents were mates, and he knew other mated couples, but they all seemed to be older than him—save one. And they'd been mated a long time. Most had met their mates years ago, some in their teens or before.

His best friend, Brett Kasper, had met his mate when he was only seventeen and she was fifteen. Brett and Poppy didn't get their fairytale ending mainly because Brett was a giant chicken shit who blew his chance with her.

Now he pretty much lurked like some creeper, longing for a woman he couldn't have because she'd gotten married and started a family with another man. A very human man. If that didn't make the kick to the balls all the worse.

Watching Brett pine for a woman for over twenty years was very sobering, and not something Jeffrey wanted to experience for himself. Seeing Brett live it was pathetic enough.

If Fate was on his side—which Jeffrey was inclined to believe was the case, seeing as how it had not put his mate in front of him in forty-two years—then he'd just keep on living the high life as a bachelor. He could toss back a beer or two, eat his fill of greasy cheeseburgers, and sleep with whomever he wanted.

"Yes, I mean married, not mated," said Gilbert, yanking Jeffrey from his thoughts. "Seeing as how you won't get a choice in the matter if your mate walks through the door."

The door opened, and in walked Noel Lawson,

a were-bear who drove a truck for a living. He'd not seen a razor in a number of years and had a beard that any member of ZZ Top would have been slightly envious of. Noel had graduated high school with Jeffrey's younger sister.

Ryan laughed hard. "Your face! You know you were secretly worried when the door opened that Fate was dropping your mate on your lap."

It's true, he was.

"Unless hairy truckers are your thing, you're safe," said Ryan, still laughing.

"You never know," added Jeffrey with a wink.

Gilbert grinned. "Notice you avoided answering my question on when you'll get married."

"A quarter to never," stated Jeffrey. It was rare to find your mate as a supernatural, and even rarer to find someone who wasn't your mate, but whom you had strong feelings for, and marry them the way humans did. Doing so meant each person in the relationship was running the risk of meeting their actual mate one day. It's why it was rarely done.

He knew a guy who had done it. The guy had thought the woman was his mate, only to learn later that magik had been used to fool his senses. A child came of the union, which was nearly unheard of, considering the pairing wasn't between a mated couple, but it was what it was.

Gilbert set his glass down and wiped the foam from his mouth with the back of his hand. "Never say never, Farkas. A woman could always blow into town any day now and knock you off your feet. Could happen."

"Highly unlikely," said Jeffrey with a shake of his head. Gilbert was starting to sound like Jeffrey's mother, who was always after him to go out into the world and find his mate. "They'd have to come in with hurricane-force winds to be able to possibly budge me."

With a laugh, Gilbert nodded. "More like a tornado. A hurricane has more lead and prep time. You need to be caught off-guard."

Jeffrey laughed. "I'll keep one eye on the forecast. If I see the threat of inclement weather, I'm going to hide in my cabin and not come out until the coast is clear."

Ryan lifted his chin slightly, giving a quick glance in Gilbert's direction.

It was easy to see something was on his mind.

"You can talk in front of Gilbert," said Jeffrey.

Gilbert might not be pack but he was trustworthy. Though Jeffrey would cut him off as far as beer soon, like he always did, and see to it Gilbert got home safe and sound. Gilbert seemed to think salvation could be found at the bottom of a bottle. While alcohol was great at numbing life's pain, it was shit at actually fixing the root of the problem. And it was a slippery slope. One that many went down but couldn't find their way back from.

Ryan cleared his throat. "I had patrol duty this evening after work. My section was the woods out near the Proctor House."

Jeffrey stiffened as his pack mate mentioned the woods. "Tell me another body wasn't found."

The town of Grimm Cove had seen a rash of unsolved murders in the last few months; tensions among the various supernatural groups had reached an all-time high. If the murders continued, human authorities would come poking their noses around where they didn't belong. There was a higher-than-likely chance that in doing so, they'd discover a truth Grimm Cove didn't want out there.

Part of Ryan's pack duties were to help with protection, and that included assisting wherever he might be needed. Right now, it was all hands on deck as the pack helped patrol the town, hoping to head off any more murders or body dumps.

Gilbert began to squirm on his barstool, looking uncomfortable with the topic.

Ryan shook his head. "No. Well, maybe, but not by me and not that I've heard about."

"Good," said Jeffrey, meaning it. Already, two pack mates had happened upon bodies. They'd done the right thing, going straight for pack help. He didn't need any more of his wolves involved if he could help it. "What's up?"

"I don't know," said Ryan before taking a drink of his beer. "Maybe nothing, but there was something different about the area near the old caves. Seemed darker than it should be. Gave me the willies too. Anyone else mention it?"

"No, but I'll let Brett know just in case," he said, making a mental note to tell his best friend, who happened to be the chief of police and a fellow pack mate.

"Did you smell anything?" asked Gilbert, perking slightly. "Anything sweet maybe?"

"Nothing sweet, but there was something," confessed Ryan.

Jeffrey watched him closely. "What was it?"

"Nothing," said Ryan.

"I'm not following," replied Jeffrey.

"I didn't smell anything," repeated Ryan. "Like

nothing. Not the woods, not the wet leaves, *nothing*. In that area, there was an absence of scents and sounds. It was eerie…or it was my imagination running away on me. Normally I'd have Robbie with me, but he's working so much here now, I barely see him. Not that I'm complaining. This place is good for him."

"Do me a favor and don't go back out to that area in the woods unless another pack mate is with you," said Jeffrey. "Might be nothing, but if it's something…"

"Understood," said Ryan, tapping the bar top. "I need to hit the head."

"Want chili?" asked Robbie from the kitchen pass-through loudly, looking out at his brother.

"Yep," said Ryan as he went in the direction of the restroom.

"Got yourself a good cook there," said Gilbert with a nod to the opening in the wall that allowed food to be passed from the kitchen to the outer bar area.

"People are loving his food," said Jeffrey. "Tried to offer him the position of manager here but he didn't want it. Seems to enjoy cooking."

"He's doing better then, since he got back?" asked Gilbert.

Jeffrey didn't like to discuss the personal business of his pack with non-pack members, but Gilbert and Robbie had a strange friendship. Though Gilbert had Robbie by a number of years, the two got along well, and Jeffrey knew Robbie often paid Gilbert's cabin a visit whenever the weather got bad, just to be sure the man didn't need anything.

And Gilbert was right. Robbie was doing better than he had been after he'd first gotten out of the military.

"Yeah, things are starting to look up for him," said Jeffrey.

Robbie had suffered something of a setback in the last few months when it came to controlling his wolf side. No one knew how or why things had gotten out of hand, but they had. Jeffrey suspected it might have something to do with his time serving overseas. It's why Jeffrey had reached out to a few of his friends who were trained to help servicemen and women with adjusting back to civilian life. They were also supernaturals, so they understood all the issues Robbie faced.

Robbie was a trusted pack member and held a pretty high ranking. The spot was in jeopardy if he couldn't get his shifter side back under control. For the time being, he was sticking close to Jeffrey, and that meant taking on a job as a cook at the bar. Turns out, the guy had a real way with short orders and was especially gifted when it came to pizza making. He'd been busy instructing the daytime cook as well, making sure the entire food game was upped at the bar.

"Robbie had been doing really good when he first got back. Then it all changed. Can I ask when his problems started?" asked Gilbert, something off in his voice. "About three months ago?"

"Just over, why?" asked Jeffrey, curious as to how the man guessed the timeframe nearly on the nose.

"No reason. Just being nosy," said Gilbert, looking a little green around the collar.

"Want me to have him make you a burger? He made chili earlier. I know you like that. I can put some in a bowl on the side," offered Jeffrey, wondering when the last time was the man had eaten actual food and hadn't just drank his calories.

Shaking his head, Gilbert focused on his beer. "Ever wish you were stronger? That what you were made of was more than it was?"

"You mean do I wish I was more alpha?" asked

Jeffrey with a snort, hoping to help lighten the mood.

Gilbert let out a shaky laugh. "Guess I'm talking to the wrong man, huh?"

"Not at all," said Jeffrey. "There are times I wish I had more mettle. That I could be what everyone thinks I should be. The prodigal son and all that shit. Why do you ask?"

Gilbert ran his finger through the condensation ring on the bar where his glass sat. "No reason. Just prying."

"You having some regrets?" asked Jeffrey, wanting to help the man any way he could.

While Gilbert wasn't a wolf-shifter, he was a shifter all the same. Granted, he was a deer-shifter, but still. That meant in some weird way, he was kin.

And shifters didn't let shifters have existential crises alone.

"If regrets were pennies, I'd be a very rich man," said Gilbert, looking defeated.

"Is everything all right with you and yours?"

Gilbert's gaze darted away. "Yes. Ruttin' season will be here before long. Not lookin' forward to it."

As a deer-shifter, Gilbert had a rough go of it from just about every group of supernaturals in

Grimm Cove. It wasn't as if being able to shift into Bambi held a lot of pull or anything.

Jeffrey was about to comment on Gilbert's rutting season worries when movement from Elis and his crew up near the front of the bar caught his attention.

His jaw set.

He really hated slayers.

Each and every last one of them.

Especially the Van Helsings.

They were the worst.

TWO

Dana

"YOU'RE NOT GETTING any younger, Dana."

Ah, there it was. The ever-faithful reminder from my ninety-year-old grandmother that I had yet to settle down and start a family. The topic wasn't new. It had been a sore point between us for the greater part of twenty years. Right about the time she'd realized that I'd gone to college to pursue a career, not a husband.

Not sure where she got the idea that I'd gone to Yale to land a man rather than a degree in law, but she had. Convincing her of anything different was a lot like trying to talk the spots off a leopard.

Wasn't going to happen.

Over the years, I'd seen her pride in what I did start to show through, especially when I made the paper for putting away a particularly bad dude, but those moments were fewer and farther between than the ones where she pushed at me to find that special someone.

That person who completed me, or whatever else song-and-dance, chick-flick movies liked to pretend happened.

As if there was such a guy.

I liked to think I did just fine completing myself. What in the hell did I need with a man?

I was particularly bitter about the male species in general because one of my two besties was going through a rather ugly divorce at the moment. Poppy had said "I do" and put in her time, only to have it end the way it did.

She'd been married for nineteen years. While I'd never been a fan of her husband, Thomas, they'd seemed happy as a couple. She got into that whole gig of being a mom and a wife. I honestly couldn't understand how or why, but it made her happy so that was all that mattered.

She'd popped out two crotch goblins, Tucker and Pepper, back at the start of her marriage, and they were now freshmen in college. They were also considerably easier to be around now that they were able to form full sentences and didn't want me to pick them up and hold them. Plus, the risk they'd wet themselves had declined dramatically over the years.

That was always nice.

Seeing Poppy's world shatter around her after Thomas announced he'd found someone new, and that he'd been sleeping around on her for the whole of their marriage, was enough to sour me to the idea of happily ever after.

Not that I wasn't already on the side of not needing a man to make my life whole.

I'll admit, there were times I wouldn't mind rolling over at night to find someone I cared about there, rather than emptiness. And there were a few times, every now and again, when I'd like to be held and told everything would be all right. But those times weren't enough to justify the heartache and complications relationships brought.

Back when I was still young and impressionable, I'd let myself fall for a guy's charms. I'd bought into his promises of a future.

Of something more.

Sure, we'd both been teens, but I'd believed in the connection we'd had. I'd trusted it and I'd trusted him. In the end, I'd gotten my heart broken.

That had been the very same day I'd left for college, and it wasn't something I talked about. Poppy and my other bestie, Marcy, knew I'd had a boyfriend all through high school and that it was serious, at least for me. They didn't know much beyond that, which was fine.

The details weren't important.

It wasn't like he was part of my life anymore.

I knew it was silly to hold the entire male population at fault for the actions of one, but the idea of daring to open my heart to another guy always left me going back to how painful it had been to be dumped. And how lonely life had seemed the following months.

That was all in the past.

I'd buried it and focused on getting a great education and landing my dream job. I was an assistant district attorney in Manhattan—the greatest city on earth. As a born-and-bred New Yorker, I loved everything about the city, and was proud to help keep it a little bit safer. And I was damn proud of all I'd achieved in my career.

Yes, I could have done it with a family, but it would have been harder, I'm sure. I saw some of my peers juggling their family lives with work responsibilities. It didn't look easy or fun, but they managed.

The most I had to worry about was checking in on Nonna Wilma, who, while opinionated on my lack of a real love life, loved me dearly. I loved her too. She was all the family I had left, and I didn't like to think about what I'd do when she was no longer with me. Her age made that possibility a daily reality. One I did my best to pretend wasn't a thing.

She was feisty, and I was fairly sure the higher-ups weren't ready to handle her up there just yet. They were probably knee-deep in preparation-readiness drills all geared toward dealing with Hurricane Nonna.

"Well, when is it you plan to settle down?" Nonna demanded as she manned her station at the stove, stirring her homemade marinara sauce with great vigor. Pavarotti's rendition of "Nessun Dorma" played in the background from a CD I'd gotten my grandmother years prior.

Try as I might to get her to move over to going fully digital with her music collection, it never panned out. I counted my win moving her from records to CDs and left well enough alone. It was better for everyone and my sanity. I just wished I could convince her to change the CDs every once in a while. It was a five-disc player, and she'd had the same five discs on rotation since I'd gotten it for her.

It was a darn shame the volume wasn't higher. It could drown out her nonstop pestering on me finding a man.

"You just turned forty, and what do you have to show for it?" she asked, as if on cue.

A fantastic career, my own apartment, a good 401k, and so on, but none of that translated into anything she'd see as value because none of them were a husband.

Generationally, we were worlds apart. It had always been that way and would always remain so. That was fine. Explaining to her my side of things never really got me far. She was a hard-headed Italian woman who wasn't about to change her mind or sway my way anytime soon.

Okay, ever.

To her, women got married when they were young. They had dinner on the table for their family by six every night and they were always dressed as if they might need to attend a nice luncheon at any random moment. They didn't forgo the man and the baby carriage for a career.

No.

That simply wasn't done.

Yet that was exactly what I'd picked. And she was quick to point out I chose the lifestyle—it didn't choose me.

My mother didn't have a choice. She had to go out and work in order to support us. My father, who I knew very little about, had passed away when I was little, leaving my mother and me on our own.

My grandmother had my grandfather's pension, which hadn't been a whole lot, and we'd gotten whatever government assistance we qualified for—which didn't go very far for a family of three in New York City. Money was always tight, probably tighter than even I realized, when I was young.

There were countless times I'd find my mother sitting at the kitchen table with her nearly empty change jar out, counting and recounting the coins as if the second, third, or even tenth time would yield different results. She never let me see her cry, but I could hear her doing it when she thought I was asleep.

She busted her butt waiting tables and serving others for pennies on the dollar. She'd worked long hours and came home with blisters on her feet in order to put food on our table. And through it all, she never let me see the toll it took on her. She kept a brave face and tried her best to make it feel as if we weren't stone-cold broke.

Back then, I didn't realize we were. No one else had much around us either so it felt normal. But my mother would sit with me on the sofa as we watched whatever sitcom was popular at the time. She'd put an arm around me, draw me closer to her, kiss the top of my head, and ask me about school and my homework.

She'd then tell me that an education was key. To get as much as I could. And when it came time to apply for colleges and scholarships, she'd sat at the table with me, going through everything, helping me fine-tune my submissions.

The pure joy on her face when she'd learned I'd been accepted into Yale was something I carried with me to this very day. The memory was strong enough and life-altering enough to help me weather a million Nonna Wilma pushes for me to have a family rather than a career.

I could still vividly recall my mother's excitement—and then the quick deflation of it when we realized the acceptance to Yale hadn't come with the full ride we'd been hoping for. I'd tempered my enthusiasm and cast Yale out of my mind, thinking it unobtainable.

Then, just days later, my mother handed me an envelope. In it was a letter telling me I'd been granted a scholarship that would not only cover my tuition and books, but room, board, and a few extras as well. While I couldn't remember applying to the foundation that had granted me the scholarship, that hadn't mattered. I'd been given my golden ticket to the education she'd always wanted for me, and I hadn't wanted to let her down.

She'd then had to deal with her mother, who, while happy for me, was not thrilled the university wasn't in New York. In fact, Nonna wasn't thrilled with a lot about the situation back then. I'd heard her and my mother arguing late one night about my scholarship. Nonna was of the opinion it had too many potential strings attached. That it opened the door to a past best left dead and buried.

To this day, I still didn't know what she'd meant by that, but my mother had. And my mother had been adamant that my education was worth the price.

So when she was ripped from this world before her time, her burning desire for me to get a formal education stuck with me. It drove me to succeed.

To get all the schooling I could and to make something of myself—for her and for me. While she'd not lived to see those dreams come to fruition, I knew deep down that wherever she was in the afterlife, she was proud.

That was enough for me.

And that alone helped me deal with Nonna's endless pushes for me to find a man and get married.

"You're not listening to me, are you?" she asked, rapping her knuckles on the side of her small stove, yanking me from my thoughts.

I smiled. "Of course, I'm listening. Would I ignore you?"

She snorted. "In a heartbeat."

The woman was barely taller than the stockpot she'd been planted in front of since my arrival nearly an hour ago. So far, I'd only been permitted to carry the pot of water for boiling pasta to the stovetop. That was where she'd drawn the line, turning the burner on herself as if I couldn't be trusted to get the temperature right. Basically, I was only good for heavy lifting in her mind.

I wasn't horrible in the kitchen. I just wasn't the culinary ninja she was. She didn't use a cookbook or follow any written recipes. Everything she did was basically muscle memory at her age. She went off sight, smell, and taste. Nothing more. And her food never disappointed.

She never seemed to tire while cooking. While I could cook—thanks to her tutelage—I didn't like to. I didn't confess that to her because it would fall along the same lines as telling her I was off pasta because of the carbs.

I'd tried that once and knew better than to attempt it again.

She'd ranted and raved for days about how she'd been raised on pasta just fine. I'd gotten so sick of hearing about it all that I drove over to her place and ate two huge bowls of it just to get her to let the topic drop.

Nonna didn't fad diet. She didn't jump on any trend. She was old-school in a lot of ways but managed to surprise me in others.

"Nonna, let me get that," I said, making a move to take the twenty-four-inch wooden spoon from her.

She eyed the spoon handle and then me as she continued to stir. Her look was all the warning I needed.

Touch the spoon at my own peril.

She was tiny but plucky. Not to mention, I was

31

pretty sure after a genealogy assignment I was handed in junior high that her side of the family had a long-standing history with the Mafia. Of course, if you asked her, she denied it and then would wink. Apparently, full-fledged Mafia members didn't like discussing it with kids for school projects.

I may have had her by a foot and was fifty years younger, but I was no dummy. I wasn't going to touch her spoon without permission. There was always the off chance she'd follow through on her threat to tan my hide. And at my age, if I was going to be spanked, I wanted it to be by a hunky guy, not my grandmother.

Putting my hands up to signal surrender, I nodded. "You don't need my help with dinner. The kitchen is your domain. Message received."

"Good," she said, appearing pleased as punch. "Now, back to you and finding a man."

I groaned. "I thought we were off that topic."

"You thought wrong," she said with a grin.

"Can we *please* talk about something else? Anything else?" I begged as I considered making a move to snatch the wooden spoon from Nonna and run through her apartment, holding it out of her reach, just to get her mind off me and men.

I highly doubted it would work, but it could totally be worth her wrath for the sheer amusement factor alone.

She shrugged. "Fine. But we will revisit this."

Oh goodie.

Nonna lifted her head slightly. "When you get a chance, will you look at the table thing again?"

By "table thing," she meant tablet. I'd long ago stopped trying to get her to understand she was saying it wrong. "What's up with it?"

"The Face-a-book is not working," she said, her Italian accent shining through. "It won't let me in. I tried the word-pass you wrote down. It didn't work."

She had a habit of keying in the passwords wrong and getting locked out.

"I'll look at it after dinner," I said.

She eyed the black dress I was wearing and gave a nod of approval. "That looks good on you. Shows your figure. You went with a support bra. Good. You're not as blessed in the chest as most women. Your dress could be a little shorter."

Nothing like being reminded I was a solid B cup. As for my dress, it came to just below my knees when I was standing and when I sat, it rode up slightly. "Nonna, it's short enough for work."

"You have such long legs. Show them off," she said, still employing her cooking genius on the sauce before her. "It would draw attention from your chest. Maybe no one will notice it then."

"My breasts are just fine, Nonna," I said, sounding as tired as the conversation made me feel. I was no Marcy in the chest area, but I held my own just fine. That being said, I found myself adjusting my bra, hoping Victoria was able to work her magik.

Nonna merely glanced at my attempt at fluffing "the girls" and then checked her pot of water. It was nearly to a rolling boil.

"I saw on television they have chicken cutlets you can put in your bra to give you more cleavage," she said.

I couldn't help but laugh. "Chicken cutlets?"

"Something that looks like them, yes," she said, nodding with great enthusiasm. "You should try them."

"To help me land a man?" I asked.

She shrugged as if that hadn't been her meaning all along.

"You do realize that all I do is work. Kind of hard to find a man there."

"Plenty of good boys from the old neighborhood have gotten railroaded through the system. You could pick one of them," she countered, as if my office made a point of seeking out people from my old neighborhood to prosecute.

We didn't.

Can I help that the "boys" she was referring to, who were really grown men, were caught up in racketeering and countless other illegal activities? I wasn't even the prosecutor assigned to their cases. Didn't matter to Nonna.

I checked my watch, wondering how late Marcy planned on being. She always made for a nice buffer between Nonna and me. Nonna often referred to herself as being a witch. The two of them would get lost in conversations about herbs and oils and whatever else it was they liked so much.

Once they'd stopped everything to make soap poppets—whatever those were. It had kept them entertained and given me time to break out my laptop to get caught up on work emails. It also kept me out of Nonna's dating crosshairs.

Her push for marriage wasn't limited to me. She also did it to Marcy, who just so happened to be unwed, but Marcy took her in stride, seeming to enjoy the meddling.

Clearly, Marcy was a stronger woman than me.

Then again, Nonna was gentler with her pushes for Marcy to find a man and settle down. I suspected it had something to do with Marcy's past. It was one we didn't bring up.

Nonna began to hum and rock her head back and forth. It was then I noticed her hair, always dyed ink-black, was styled slightly different from her usual way. It suited her.

"I like your hair. It's styled different but it looks very nice on you," I said, noticing she had on the red sweater I'd gotten her for her birthday. The one she'd informed me would be saved for a special occasion. "You're awfully gussied up for dinner with Marcy and me."

"Am I?" she asked coyly. That meant she was up to something. "You never know who may be stopping by."

I groaned. "You didn't fix me up with someone, did you?"

"I would never," she said.

"Liar," I returned. "You've already tried fixing me up how many times in the past?"

She laughed. "Too many to count. You find something wrong with every one of them. You're impossible to please. At your age, you should be less picky."

"Anyone ever tell you that you're a real confidence booster?" I asked sardonically.

"No," she said with all honesty. "Never."

Shocking.

"I wonder what's keeping Marcy," I said, checking my watch again, desperate for her arrival to help give my grandmother a new target.

Anyone who knew Marcy and me wondered how it was we were friends at all with as opposite as we were. I was a ball-busting assistant district attorney, and she was whatever the ether told her to be at the moment. At last check, that was a yoga instructor, but a few months back it was a massage therapist; before that it was working for an online psychic service.

The list went on and on.

We'd met my freshman year of college when I'd gone off to Yale. It had been hard for me to leave the island of Manhattan. It had been my everything. All I'd ever known. And I'd been incredibly close with my mother and grandmother. The idea of leaving them both to head off to Yale, of all places, had scared the crap out of me (not that I'd have confessed as much out loud).

I'd arrived on the scene, went to my assigned residential college dorm, found my suite, and met my roommates. The suite was made for four occupants, with two per bedroom and a center shared common area. While there had been four of us to start with, Marcy had managed to scare off the girl sharing her room just one night into the ordeal.

Oddly, the university never filled the slot. So it had been only three of us from then on out.

Perfect.

We'd remained close for twenty years, becoming like sisters to one another.

Poppy lived in California. I lived in New York City. And Marcy lived wherever the wind blew her. Right now, the wind had her in New York. I'd offered my apartment to her as a place to crash but she'd refused, staying with a manfriend of hers. I wasn't about to judge her. After all, I'd seen the guy, and I wouldn't kick him out of my bed for eating crackers.

Marcy had a way of attracting very handsome men but never seeming to notice as much. It was part of her charm.

Her charm had worn a bit in the last several days, as she'd been on a kick for me to learn to channel my anger issues and release them. She seemed to think deep breathing would do the trick. That, and lighting incense that made me cough and choke.

Nonna stirred the sauce, and I caught the scent of basil and garlic—all things that made me think of her and of growing up. "It shouldn't be that a grandmother has more male suitors than her granddaughter. If you were nicer to men, they might want to ask you out more."

That made me chuckle. "I'm nice-ish and I date."

"Is that what you call what you do?" she asked, arching a brow in judgment. "Norma told me all about the walk of shame. How many times have you done this walk?"

"Nonna, why would your friend be talking about walks of shame?" I asked, unsure I wanted to know.

"Because she had one after her night with Chester," said Nonna matter-of-factly, as if that sort of thing was common behavior for a woman only two years her junior.

It took everything I had to keep from cracking up as I got a mental image of Norma holding her shoes in her hands as she tried to quietly shuffle out of Chester's room without anyone noticing.

I swear there were some people in the building who camped out near their peepholes, never missing a beat. Very little happened in the building without everyone hearing about it by the next day.

"I thought Chester and Shirley were an item," I said, having a vested interest in the topic. I visited my grandmother twice a week and always got all the juicy gossip.

Nonna waved a hand in the air dismissively. "No. Shirley was playing stuff the cannoli with George."

I gasped. "No. After all that time she spent trying to catch Chester's eye?"

My grandmother nodded. "She was only in it for the chase. After that, the thrill was gone. It was on to the next poor sap. Now George is with Rita."

"But Rita is married to Lou," I countered.

Nonna glanced at me. "They're trying something called an open marriage. Have you ever heard of such a thing? And Lou has an oxygen tank he has to wheel around with him all the time now. He says it gives him more stamina. I just think it means he has to avoid open flames, but what do I know?"

"This place is better than a daytime soap opera," I said, meaning every word of it.

Though it was kind of sad that my grandmother and her cronies got more action than I did. In my defense, I worked long hours and didn't put much stock in the whole relationship thing. If I had the urge for sex, I hooked up with a man for a night, maybe two. Nothing more. I made that clear going into it all.

No strings.

No walks of shame.

When I left, it was with my head held high.

I owned my sexuality.

"There is rarely a dull moment around here," she admitted. "Just wait until I tell you about Betsy's granddaughter and the man she ran off with."

"Stop. I'm not sure I can take all of these developments in one sitting," I said with a smile.

"I'll save that one for another visit," she said.

"What about you?" I asked. "Are you playing stuff the cannoli with anyone?"

She blushed. "No. But I do have a gentleman caller. He's newer to the building."

"Tell me more," I said, grabbing for the small bowl of shaved mozzarella cheese on the counter. I popped a piece into my mouth.

Mischief filled Nonna's face. "His name is Peter Beard."

"How unfortunate for him," I said, partially under my breath.

She kept stirring, used to my quips.

After my mother's passing while I was in college, Nonna had decided she wanted to live in a community of people her own age. She'd told me about three places in the city that her friends said were good senior centers, offering independent and assisted-living options, and I went with her to look at each. That had been twenty years ago.

She'd been here ever since.

In the span of two decades, she'd developed a tight-knit group of friends in her building, each looking after the other, on top of a trained staff available at all hours should the need arise.

The only thing I didn't like about having her in a senior center was that each time I talked to her, it seemed as if someone else had died. Though it never bothered her. At least not that she showed me. Then again, she'd always handled death differently from most.

She went to the small drawer near the stove and pulled out a silver soup spoon. She then gathered some sauce from the pot and held the spoon out for me to have a taste.

Having played the role of faithful sauce sidekick hundreds of times in my life, I knew my job well. At six feet tall in my stocking feet, I had to bend a good deal to be at her level, especially since I was a foot taller than her.

I tasted the sauce and knew better than to lie. She'd know. "Needs salt."

"Good girl," she said, as if she'd been testing me. She then placed the soup spoon in the sink and returned to her post at the stockpot.

I groaned. "Nonna, for the billionth time, just because I work around criminals every day doesn't mean they're corrupting me. I can be trusted."

"It's not the criminals I worry about," she said, her voice even. "It's the other attorneys. Lawyers. They're smooth talkers. Full of empty promises. Silver-tongued devils. The lot of them. You saw what they did to the neighborhood boys."

I let her continue her one-woman diatribe on all the ways lawyers were the root of all evil. When she finished, I looked down at her. "You do realize I'm a lawyer, right?"

"You don't count," she said, adding a touch of salt to the sauce as she stirred.

"Thanks. I think."

"You didn't answer me about finding a man and settling down," said Nonna.

I was hoping she'd forgotten about that.

No such luck.

"We've gone over this before," I said, already tired, and the topic had just started up again. "I don't have time to date."

"Make time," she said as if it were that easy. "You should take a vacation."

"And go where and do what?" I asked.

She shrugged. "Maybe go to South Carolina."

"What?" I was honestly shocked she even knew there was a state called South Carolina. The woman had come over from Italy when she was younger, arrived in New York City, and there she had remained. She didn't travel off the island much, if ever, anymore. To her, everything she needed in the world was in the radius of a few blocks, and the world beyond that was pointless.

I'd tried to take her back to Italy for Christmas one year and you'd have thought I'd threatened to give her secret sauce recipe out on the internet with the way she'd reacted. I'd assumed she'd be thrilled to visit her homeland.

"Why on earth would you suggest South

Carolina as a place for me to vacation?" I asked with a slight laugh, picturing myself in the South. I'd stick out like a sore thumb.

She focused on her sauce in a way that said she was up to something. "No reason other than the time has come."

The time had come? What did she mean by that?

"Nonna, what are you up to?" I asked.

Nonna put pasta in the boiling water and ignored my question.

There was a knock on the door, and I couldn't have gotten to it faster if I tried. Tossing the door open, I came face-to-face with someone who wasn't Marcy. Unless Marcy had suddenly turned into a man who looked to be my grandmother's age.

The man stood there in a suit that was a little loose on him, as if it had been from a day when he had more bulk than he did now. He held a bouquet of flowers in his hands and looked nervous. The top of his head was shiny and totally absent of hair. Most of it seemed to have migrated to the sides of his head and his ears.

"You must be Dana," he said, squaring his shoulders and standing tall. Well, as tall as his five-foot, five-inch frame would allow.

I stared down at him and realized why it was my grandmother was so gussied up. She'd planned the dinner so that I could meet the new man in her life. "And you must be Peter."

He gave a curt nod. "I am. It was so nice of Wilma to arrange this dinner. I've been asking to meet you for weeks now. I ran into your friend down the street when I was getting flowers. She said to tell you she can't make it to dinner tonight but to try to remember to work on your breathing exercises."

I was going to have words with Marcy later for abandoning me in my hour of need.

I held the door open for him. "Come on in, Peter. We can discuss your intentions with my grandmother."

THREE

Jeffrey

_____

THE DOOR to the bar opened and in walked a tall man with dark hair. Brett was in full uniform and everything about him screamed law enforcement. It didn't hurt that his badge and name tag announced as much too. He was the chief of police in Grimm Cove, and just so happened to be Jeffrey's best friend since basically birth. On top of that, Brett was also pack enforcer. That meant when there was a pack issue, Brett handled Jeffrey's wishes. He was the muscle behind the rule of law.

Brett's presence drew the attention of all the slayers at the table, and they stopped laughing and carrying on, choosing instead to watch him carefully. They weren't as stupid as they looked. They knew Brett was a wild card.

And while Jeffrey was a force to be reckoned with, when Brett was by his side, he was nearly unstoppable.

Brett's dark gaze landed on the slayers. There it remained for a long, pregnant pause. No one said a word as Brett stared at the slayers and they, in turn, stared right back at him. A few of the slayers looked a little green around the collar at the sight of Brett.

Brett had a look about him that announced he was lethal. It had always been that way. His enforcer side leaked off him as well, putting other supernaturals on blast. As a general rule, enforcers of any shifter pack, be it wolves or whatever, were typically known for having short fuses. Brett's was longer than most but that wasn't saying much.

Alphas were different. Some wore their position on their sleeve for all to know and fear. Most didn't. What was the point? Like Jeffrey, they pulled out that side of themselves when the need arose. Jeffrey looked at being an alpha a lot like having a hard-on. If he walked around with a stiff one in his pants all the time, it was uncomfortable for him and just about anyone else he happened upon. But if he had it when needed—well, it could be one hell of a good time.

One of the slayers slid back slightly in his chair, giving Brett wide berth. The action left Elis grunting at the man and sending a scathing look in the slayer's direction. Clearly, he didn't like seeing any of his men backing down to a shifter.

Jeffrey hid his laugh.

Brett's gaze slid over the bar to Jeffrey. He quirked a brow as if to ask if he should make a scene.

It was on the tip of Jeffrey's tongue to tell him to go for it.

He resisted.

For now.

It would be something to watch though. Then again, it would leave the bar trashed and more than likely do hundreds if not thousands of dollars' worth of damage. Fights broke out often enough as it was. It was early in the year, and he didn't need to go burning through his backup fix-it fund so soon.

Jeffrey noticed the rest of the shifters in the bar all watching him as well, waiting for the green light to kick some slayer backside.

For half a second, he considered burning through that special fund after all, but held back.

Austin Van Helsing, younger cousin to Elis,

stood and raised his bottle of beer in Brett's direction. He wasn't quite thirty yet and had a lot of learning and growing up to do still. "Let's drink to too much testosterone and needing monthly flea dips."

Brett's jaw set, but he continued walking to the bar. He got there and put his palms on the bar top. "I'm fine with breaking that one in half if you want."

Tensions had already been high in the supernatural community because of the rash of murders happening in the area.

Austin had only just gotten back in town. He'd been gone for months, which had been glorious. The rumor mill had him in New York for a bit and then California. Too bad he'd not taken the rest of his family and buddies with him and stayed gone.

"Hold off for now," said Jeffrey. "But if you can't restrain yourself, start with eating Elis. If you have any room left, Austin is fair game."

Brett snorted. "Sounds like a plan."

It was late for Brett to be just getting off work. "You can't keep burning the candle at both ends."

Brett rotated his neck as he sighed. "I wish that was true, but I don't have a choice. We're up to eight bodies already, and we have nothing more to go off of than we had three months back when we found the first one."

"I know, and I also know you're spending every waking moment fixated on the murders. Yes. They're serious. Yes. They can bring a whole lot of shit down on our heads if the humans come nosing around, but you still need to take care of you."

"I'm taking care of me," Brett snapped.

Jeffrey let his friend have a moment. "Really? You missed this month's pack meeting. That means you missed the pack run. You know as well as I do that denying your wolf too long and not letting it free to run leads to bad things happening."

"I'm fine," said Brett, his voice deepening. That meant he was anything but fine. "I just need to find the sick bastard who is killing people and put an end to this."

"You will, but only if you make sure to see to your needs—and those of your wolf," warned Jeffrey. "It won't do any of us any good if you lose control somewhere and shift forms in public all because you've been denying your wolf what it needs."

"I know," said Brett, annoyance evident.

"You can not like the truth all you want. Doesn't make it any less true," said Jeffrey.

Brett tipped his head in Gilbert's direction. "Could this scolding have waited until we were in private?"

"Maybe. Maybe not," stated Jeffrey evenly. "I'm seeing so little of you lately that who knows when I'd get a second to mention it again."

"As soon as we catch this bastard, I'll take some vacation time," said Brett.

Jeffrey didn't like having to pull rank on Brett, but it was clear that might be needed. "No. You'll take a day off soon or I'll tranq your ass."

"How about you stay away from my backside," said Brett with a grin.

Gilbert laughed from the end of the bar, letting them know he was listening in on the conversation.

Most of the shifters there probably were as well. They had hearing that was far superior to that of a human's. That was fine. The message was one they all needed to hear. If they tried to deny what they were born with for too long, it would come back to bite them—and possibly others.

The risk of what could happen if a shifter lost control was far greater than the risk of Brett being unavailable for a day while he took some much-needed rest and relaxation time.

Austin made another loud, snide comment

from the other side of the bar.

Brett's gaze darkened. "If you change your mind, I'm totally fine with eating him first. I know how much you love the Van Helsing clan. Them being one less wouldn't break your heart any."

It was true, especially since his sister ran off with one of them. Jeffrey lifted his hands and cracked his knuckles, needing to let out some tension.

"Jennifer still hasn't reached out to your parents?" asked Brett.

Jeffrey shook his head at the mention of his sister. He didn't want to get into it all right now. "No."

Brett sighed. "She'll turn up when she's good and ready. Not a moment sooner. She has the famous Farkas temper. I swear you Hungarians have some serious rage issues."

That made Jeffrey snort. "As opposed to you? How about we talk about Poppy living it up out in California with that fancy-pants husband you keep telling me about? Let's see what happens then."

Just like that, it was as if someone had flipped a switch in the wolf-shifter. He snarled and jerked his head to one side unnaturally, an indication the beast was close to rising fully.

Jeffrey knew that he'd been right about Brett denying his shifter side for too long. He also knew he'd pushed too far while making his point by using Poppy as an example.

Poppy was Brett's mate. At least she would have been, had his best friend not had his head shoved up his ass way back when they were dating. Instead of claiming her like he should have, Brett freaked out, ran out on her, called everything off, and basically watched her from afar for nearly twenty years now.

Nothing weird about that.

Jeffrey's wolf rose to the occasion, pushing up in him, causing his eyes to go from royal blue to an icy light blue. He growled, the sound making his chest reverberate. It was the sound of an alpha warning one of his pack members to remember who was in charge.

Truth be told, Jeffrey wasn't so sure he could take Brett in a fight, and he was hoping he wouldn't have to find out. They'd been friends since birth, and their fathers had held the same positions in the pack as the two males did now. They were closer than close, and a fight for leadership could change all that.

Brett had shown zero interest in wanting the

position of pack alpha in the past, but if Jeffrey kept poking the wolf, so to speak, about Poppy, there was a high likelihood that would all change.

Jeffrey grabbed a bottle of whiskey and a glass. He filled the glass three fingers high and slid it across the bar top at Brett. "Peace offering."

Brett glanced down at his uniform.

Rolling his eyes, Jeffrey snorted. "No one cares that you're wearing the uniform or that you just got off duty, Kasper. They all know how many hours you've been putting in on the murders. Drink up. You'll need it to wash the smell of slayers out of your mouth. They smell so bad you can practically taste it."

That made Brett laugh.

Ryan returned from the restroom with a look that said no one would want to be visiting the area anytime soon—at least until it aired out. He glanced around the bar, noting the tension. "What did I miss? Robbie, what did you do?"

"Wasn't me!" shouted Robbie from the back. "This time. The culprit is up front."

Austin's first cousin, Brian Van Helsing, joined him in standing. The two shared a look before Brian went to the jukebox and fed it coins. "Dirty Deeds" filled the bar, and while Jeffrey normally liked the song and was a big AC/DC fan, he knew it was a message from the slayer to him.

You need to have Brett do your dirty work.

"Anyone else smell dog piss in here?" asked Brian loudly. "Think they've been marking their territory again?"

"Nah," said Austin. "That's not the smell of them marking their territory. It's the smell of fear. Makes 'em piss themselves, like little nervous, yappy dogs."

The rest of the slayers joined in laughing and carrying on about the wolves being nothing more than little dogs.

"Hold my drink," said Brett, thrusting his glass of whiskey in Jeffrey's direction.

Having only just gotten the man calmed, Jeffrey knew the combination of the song, the slayers, and the dig about Poppy being married was a recipe for disaster. That being said, he was in the mood to blow off some steam, and if the slayers were feeling froggy, he'd jump.

He set the drink aside and leapt over the bar, clearing it with ease. Landing crouched slightly, he set his sights on Elis.

The entire group of slayers all came up from their seats quickly.

So did all the shifters in the bar—Gilbert included.

Damn. The were-deer has spunk.

Jeffrey nodded to his men and knew they'd follow his unspoken direction—take the fight outside, to save on damaging the bar, and put the slayers in their place.

The men slammed into one another and the shifters basically rushed the slayers out the front door that just so happened to open for them.

When Jeffrey caught sight of the older woman who was holding the door open, he knew what was about to happen; he just hoped he had enough time to get a few good licks in before the fun stopped.

"Sorry, Maria!" he yelled on his way past the head of the Council of Elders. "But a wolf's gotta do what a wolf's gotta do."

"Boys," she said with a roll of her eyes and a shake of her head as she continued to hold the door open. "Just came to tell you about a storm that is headed your way."

Jeffrey turned partially to look at her, sure he'd heard her wrong. There were no storms predicted for the area that he'd heard of. "Come again?"

Just then, someone sucker punched him in the

jaw. It hurt, but what hurt more was his pride. Had he been focused, that wouldn't have happened.

His head whipped around and with one punch, he sent the young slayer to the ground before glancing at Maria again.

"You all right?" she asked. Her dress was pale yellow and her shoes matched. There was a clutch, its handle resting partway up her right arm, that was just a few shades darker than her dress. Her dark, curly hair came just shy of her shoulders and had white sprinkled throughout.

The woman looked as though she were about to attend a fancy luncheon, not stop by his bar. As a full witch, she wasn't his normal clientele, not to mention Maria wasn't exactly known for cutting loose and having drinks anywhere, let alone his bar.

He wasn't quite sure of her age, but if he had to guess he'd say she had to be in her eighties. Maybe older. She'd simply always been around for the whole of his life.

"Watch yourself." She pointed to something behind him, and he spun to catch the fist of another slayer in midair.

Brett roared and yanked the man away from Jeffrey before lifting the guy and tossing him like a rag doll. "No cheap shots on my alpha!"

"No breaking anything on anyone!" shouted Maria.

Jeffrey knew all the men who were present would listen. The witch might be up there in years, but her magik was powerful, and so was her temper when provoked. If she got the notion to make them listen, she'd do it. He'd seen her in action before and it was something indeed.

"Yes, ma'am," said Brett with a grin and a wink in her direction. "Looking as lovely as ever, Ms. Maria."

She grinned, having always had something of a soft spot for Brett. "Why thank you, Brett. Now, duck."

He did, and just missed taking a fist to the face. He flashed another smile in Maria's direction and then rushed into the commotion of the fight.

Maria pointed to Jeffrey. "You do realize the council will be left no choice but to make some serious changes around here, right?"

Biting his lower lip, he nodded. "Yes, ma'am."

Totally worth it.

She laughed. "Is it really worth it?"

His eyes widened. She read minds?

He took a foot to the back of his thigh and

nearly went down, looking over his shoulder to find it was one of his own guys.

They looked at him sheepishly. "Sorry!"

The brawl continued with shifters pitted against slayers. Everywhere you looked, there were men going at it—Jeffrey included. Before long, he felt the heavy weight of someone's stare on him and glanced in Maria's direction to find the rest of the Council of Elders standing there, looking anything but amused by what was happening.

Jeffrey's father stood next to Maria, his mouth set in a thin line.

Maria was the only Elder who was smiling.

Knowing they'd pushed too far, Jeffrey put two fingers in his mouth and whistled loudly to get everyone's attention. It worked. All the men stopped fighting.

Elis made his way over near Jeffrey, his hair disheveled, but otherwise unharmed.

Shame.

"Looks like we're in trouble," he said, with a nod of his head toward the Council of Elders.

Jeffrey said nothing.

His father grunted. "Really, boys?"

Elis leaned slightly in Jeffrey's direction. "He's talking to you."

"I'm talking to all of you," corrected Jeffrey's father, his voice deep.

Maria lifted a hand and magik trickled over the area, settling on Jeffrey's skin, making him shiver. "Now that we have your attention."

Jeffrey braced for whatever it was they were going to do next.

Maria pointed to Ryan Helens and Austin Van Helsing. "You two will do nicely."

"For?" asked Austin, earning him a harsh look from Elis.

Austin wisely shut up.

Maria glanced at the rest of the council and then back to Ryan and Austin. "Austin, I'm told Wolf's Moon Bar & Grill is in need of a manager. You'll work perfectly."

Jeffrey opened his mouth to protest, but the expression on his father's face left the words dying on his lips before they came out. It didn't matter that Jeffrey owned the bar; when Maria spoke, people obeyed.

"And you," said Maria to Ryan, "will do well to fit the opening at The Summons Law Firm."

Ryan shot a desperate look in Jeffrey's direction.

"No way!" shouted Robbie.

Maria quirked a brow.

Robbie took a step back. "Never mind. You can have him."

"Gee, thanks," said Ryan.

Maria nodded and smiled sweetly. "Additional changes are on the horizon, gentlemen. For now, this will work. And just so you all know, these changes are effective immediately."

"Shit," said Ryan partially under his breath.

Austin grunted. "What he said."

Maria set her sights on Jeffrey. "Be warned, a tornado is coming."

With that, she walked away, taking the rest of the Elders with her.

"I say we drink," said Gilbert, dusting himself off. "Who is with me?"

Every man present raised their hands.

Brett laughed. "Look at that, we're getting along."

"Bite me, fleabag," said one of the slayers.

Brett growled.

Jeffrey groaned. "Enough. If we keep pushing our luck, Maria might fuse Elis and me together mystically for a month or something to *make* us get along."

"Oh hell no," said Elis fast. "I can't stand you."

"Feeling is mutual there, buddy," said Jeffrey.

FOUR

Dana

"I SWEAR, Marcy, if you don't get that tree-rat out of here, I'm going to skin it and wear it as a hat," I said in a hushed whisper as I held a running shoe in one hand, pointing it at a small gray rodent with a black face and bushy tail. The tiny creature leapt from its cozy sleeping position, which just so happened to be inside one of my designer knee-high black leather boots, and took off running.

It zipped through the room I'd be calling my own until I had the time and inclination to find my own place. Since the bedroom currently came completely furnished and with its own squirrel, my motivation to begin house hunting ramped up significantly. It had already been high on my priority list, especially with as crowded as the old Victorian home was getting.

Not to mention the house Poppy's grandparents had left her was far more than met the eye. Everything in Grimm Cove was. And Proctor House was just one more shining example of the twilight zone I'd stepped into since arriving in South Carolina.

Apparently, the house held a wealth of actual power. Real magik. The kind most people assumed only existed in fairy tales and movies. Forty-eight hours ago, it was the same kind of magik I'd assumed wasn't real.

Oh, how wrong I'd been.

When I'd said yes to giving up my career and apartment back in New York, and moving with my besties to Grimm Cove, it was with the understanding that I'd be sharing Poppy's grandparents' old home with her and Marcy, and Poppy's two children in the summers, until we got settled or longer.

At no point did anyone mention her dearly departed grandparents' ghosts would be inhabiting it along with us—or that ghosts were even real, for that matter. Poppy's fraternal grandparents, Tucker (Tuck) and Ellie-Sue Proctor, were hardly dead and gone. They were dead and here.

That was still taking some getting used to on my part.

I'd only just met Ellie-Sue, though I'd heard a lot about her from Poppy over the years. I'd even sent flowers to her funeral some two years back. Cue my struggle with coming to grips with the fact I'd already had several lovely sit-down discussions with her in the last two days.

Hanging with ghosts was becoming a regular occurrence for me, and I wasn't sure how I felt about that. Ellie-Sue didn't look dead when she was around. She was itty-bitty and tender-hearted. Her Southern accent was nearly as adorable as she was. And her sayings left me biting back a laugh more often than not.

As for Tuck, the other resident spirit in the Proctor House, he'd taken to showing himself to me often since his first apparitional coming-out just over forty-eight hours prior, when an honest-to-God succu-bitch (succubus who was also part witch, yet total bitch) and her evil minions tried to kill me and my best friends.

The skank had some sort of magik va-jay-jay that apparently ensnared men with ease. Part of me was jealous. The other was thankful it wasn't catching. I didn't need or want my vag acting like the Pied Piper.

Thanks, but I had enough issues all on my own. I didn't need that added to it all.

Tuck had a few choice words about Darla (okay, fine, Marla) and how she'd broken up his grand-daughter's marriage, and he'd been vocal in sharing them with me. He, like myself, was torn. On one hand, he was pleased Poppy wasn't married to Thomas any longer, but on the other, he knew Thomas's infidelity had hurt Poppy deeply. The succu-bitch had used Thomas as a means to get closer to Poppy in hopes of being able to drain her magik, like she'd done to many others, leaving them dead. But that hadn't gone as planned with Poppy. Instead, the succu-witch had gotten her ass handed to her and gone poof into a plume of green smoke.

That happened right after Darla the succu-bitch had sent her evil thralled vampire followers after us all. Tuck had shown himself then, revealing that, while he was dead, he was not in fact gone.

His ghostly coming-out had occurred in a dramatic fashion, complete with him wearing a sheet and freaking me out, right before knocking over two bad guys in the fight to end all fights.

Once I got past the fact the guy was dead, yet could appear to be totally not dead, I found I had a lot in common with him. He had a dark wit about him that I related well to. He'd been very helpful in explaining the finer points of the supernatural world to me since I was brand-spanking new to it all.

Turns out not all vampires are evil. At least according to Tuck. And there are so many types of shifters that listing them would be nearly impossible. There were handwritten books that were in the study. He'd shown them to me and, so far, the information within had been nothing short of eye-opening.

I'd been riveted by them, but for as fascinating as I found them to be, they also freaked me out. Had I read them prior to knowing the truth about supernaturals, I'd have still been interested in them, but I wouldn't have believed a word they said. Knowing they spoke the truth, and that I'd only just scratched the surface of what was out there, was weighing heavily on me.

Everything in my life had flipped upside down forty-eight hours ago, and I felt like I was doing my best to keep my head above water.

Poppy was handling the seemingly nonstop revelations with style and grace. Typical Poppy.

Marcy didn't seem the least bit fazed by anything that had happened. It was as if she'd known the truth all along. Typical Marcy.

The last thing I wanted to do was alert either of them to the fact I was having a hard time dealing with everything. This was supposed to be a happy, joyous time for us.

The three of us were starting over. Taking life in our forties by the balls and making it our bitch.

Or so had been the plan.

At this point, I wasn't sure who or what was in charge of the second part of my life, but it certainly didn't feel like it was me.

I'd had a trial-by-fire introduction to supernaturals and was still doing my best to come to terms with everything.

It was a lot.

A whole lot.

But I was doing my best, and right now my best also included dealing with a small rodent that I'd found in one of my boots—again. "Get out of here, fur-ball."

It darted behind a stack of cardboard boxes I had yet to unpack and then skittered underneath the empty ones once again. The empty ones toppled and filled the open doorway, looking as if an earthquake had occurred.

I thought that was the end of the squirrel, but the darn thing raced back into my room, making the already fallen boxes topple more. He shot past the full boxes, and I reached out quickly to steady them as I let out a long-annoyed breath. "Marcy, you're about to be one tree-rat short of a nut-bunch if you don't get your butt in here and deal with him."

Marcy strolled into my room, seeming downright bored by my theatrics.

The sun had yet to rise, but she was fully dressed and looked to have been up for some time already.

Wearing clothing that looked as if she might try to dance barefoot around a bonfire right before telling my fortune, she pushed her way through the toppled boxes, looking like the hippie version of Godzilla invading my bedroom.

The heavy scent of jasmine and sage followed her, and I had to wonder what she'd been doing only moments before. If I knew her, she'd been down mixing potions or some other nonsense in what we'd taken to calling the green room, which was just off the kitchen.

It was basically a witch's wet dream, and Marcy spent most of her time in there, sorting through everything, doing who knows what. She also came out smelling like she could clear a room of negative energy by simply exhaling.

"Is there a problem?" she asked.

I held up my running shoe. "I'm planning to use this as a deadly weapon in a minute. I'm undecided if it's you I'm killing or your pet tree-rat."

Waving a hand in front of my face in an attempt to get the overwhelming scent of sage away from me, I watched as she scrambled to get the very rodent I'd only just been chasing.

The bracelets she wore on each arm, stopping a few inches from her elbows, clanged loudly. The faster she tried to find the very fast rodent, the more noise the bracelets made. She was like a one-man band. She wore three different necklaces, each one longer than the next. They made as much noise as the bracelets, if not more.

If her goal was ever being stealthy, she'd fail miserably.

I wore a simple silver chain with a matching small cross that had been a gift for my Catholic confirmation from my mother when I was in eighth grade.

That was it.

But not Marcy.

No.

She jingled and jangled with every movement.

I'd heard cowbells make less ruckus than she did.

Finally, she ceased making noise, but that was only because she stopped trying to catch her pet squirrel. She bit at her lower lip, and it was evident she knew she was in deep shit with me. "Sorry. I thought he was sleeping in my room. Are you heading out for a morning run? You always liked those in New York. You'll love it down here. Fresh air. Scenery. So relaxing and refreshing. You can practice your breathing exercises too—you know, for your temper."

"Your tree-rat was in my boot—again," I said, going for my designer pair of black boots and lifting one for her to get the full effect of my annoyance.

The little fur-ball picked then to show itself once more as it poked its head out from under the end of my dresser. For as irritated as I was with the small thing, even I had to admit it looked adorable as it did something close to a tiptoe in Marcy's direction.

I rethought the whole "using my running shoe as a weapon" thing.

Marcy bent and put her hand out, holding her head high as if she were truly offended. "Burgess is not a rat, Dana. He's a Southern fox squirrel, and he doesn't like it when you say mean things about him and threaten him. He understands that you won't really harm him and that your frustration with him comes from another place, not one of real anger, but it still hurts his feelings. He wishes you would speak to him from a place of love. Not a place of aggression."

Aggression?

I'd give the little fur-ball aggression.

"I don't like it when he climbs in my boots and decides to nest or nap, or whatever it is tree-rats do," I said, holding up my boot again. "And I wish he'd go live in a tree, where he belongs. There. Said with love."

The sugary-sweet smile I offered should have been the icing on top. Knowing Marcy, she'd miss the not-so-subtle hint that I wanted to call animal control on her pet.

Just then, Burgess scrambled up her chest and

came to a seat on her shoulder, of all places, right by her face.

Horrified, I gasped. "Marcy, that thing could have rabies."

"Highly unlikely," she said, turning her head and puckering her lips in its direction.

I stood there, frozen, holding one running shoe, as I watched my friend give a squirrel a quick, chaste kiss.

"Who is a good little boy?" she asked in a high-pitched voice. "That's right. You are."

"Ohmygod, you put your lips on it!"

She rolled her eyes. "You're very dramatic."

"This from a woman who hugs trees and kisses rodents," I snapped.

FIVE

Dana

_____

"TRY to be more patient with him," Marcy implored, her bottom lip jutting out as she reached up and stroked Burgess, who was still on her shoulder. "He's learning to be a house squirrel. It's difficult on him. We need to all remember to be kind and to show restraint when dealing with him."

I inwardly counted to ten, hoping it would help my level of irritation with both the tree-rat and my friend.

It didn't work.

I clutched my running shoe tighter.

"Here's the thing, Marcy. He's not a _house_ squirrel. He's a wild animal that belongs outside," I argued. "He can play with all the other tree-rats out there. You know, join in all the fun tree-rat games. Be part of their boys' club. Whatever. You'd be doing him a favor. Set him free."

"I'm not holding him here against his will," she said quickly. "He wants to be here."

I lifted a brow. "Why? Does he have a thing for Italian leather? It's the only explanation I have for why he keeps crawling into my boots."

She drew the squirrel close to her very blessed chest and lowered her lips to the top of its head. "Ignore her. She hasn't had any coffee yet this morning and she didn't go for her morning run yet. I, for one, think coffee is poison, but she loves it and is addicted. And without it, she's *barely* a house-human. After several very large cups, she is only nearly human. And if she doesn't run daily, she's extra cranky. Oh, maybe you could go on her run with her. What a fun bonding experience!"

"*Forgetaboutit*," I said, knowing my New Yorker was shining through. To non-New Yorkers, I probably sounded like a gangster. I was totally fine with that. There was no way in hell I was going for a run with that thing.

The squirrel squeaked and clucked at her as if it was part dog toy and part Morse code machine. Whatever it said, Marcy seemed to understand.

That, or she did a great job making me think she did, with all the nodding and animated facial expressions. She also had in-depth conversations with trees and just about any kind of flora or fauna one could find. It wasn't really new for her. She'd always been an odd duck.

When Marcy finally stopped with the theatrics, she looked me dead in the eyes. "Burgess says he'll stay out of your boots if you'll let him sleep in your dirty clothes hamper. Seems like a fair trade. What say you?"

I focused on the tree-rat and shocked myself by not lunging for the thing. "Tell him I'll let him *live* if *he* stays out of my room."

She sighed and stared down at the squirrel that she insisted came with the name Burgess. When we'd arrived in town, she'd met the squirrel in the side yard of the house we were staying in. The two had apparently hit it off well, seeing as how he was now a permanent fixture at the Proctor House and in my boot.

After a few clucks, squeaks, and general weird-ness back-and-forth with Burgess, Marcy focused on me. "He says it's a deal. He would like to compliment your hard-nosed negotiation tactics. He thinks you're going to make a great attorney here in Grimm Cove, and he's frankly ecstatic you're finally here. You, me, and Poppy have been all the buzz around here with the flora and fauna."

She was so freaking weird.

"Glad to have his stamp of approval. Means the world to me." I rolled my eyes. "Take him with you when you leave."

She stroked the animal's head gently. "He's my familiar. You need to get along with him, Dana Van Helsing."

It was serious if she was using my full name to scold me. I bit back a laugh at just how nonintimidating the woman was. I was more scared of Burgess than her. "I have no idea what you're talking about."

"He's my *familiar*," she stressed, as if speaking slower would suddenly make it clearer to me.

It didn't. I had no earthly idea what a familiar was, only that she'd mentioned it more than a few times since we'd gotten to Grimm Cove.

"You do know what a familiar is, don't you?" she asked, surprise lifting her brows.

I shrugged. "Got nothing here, and you repeating it doesn't equal me understanding it any better."

"How is it you have a grandmother who is a

witch, yet you are so utterly clueless about every-thing and anything to do with them?" she ques-tioned with nothing but sincerity in her voice.

I stiffened at the mention of my grandmother. "Nonna Wilma isn't a real witch. I mean, she fancies herself something of one, but she's not like you and Poppy."

I'd seen firsthand the actual power my best friends possessed just days prior. We'd locked hands and turned the succu-bitch into nothing more than stinky, sulfur-smelling green smoke. Much to my surprise, I'd gotten past the initial shock of that rather quickly and moved right into stunned-stupid territory.

I'd then proceeded to channel my inner turmoil into something I saw as productive. That was cleaning. I'd spent most of the last twenty-four hours scouring every surface I could find, avoiding talking to anyone about anything of substance as I ran my new reality through my head on a loop.

Everyone had been good about giving me space when they saw I needed it.

Well, everyone except Burgess.

He seemed hell-bent on bunking with me by way of my expensive Italian leather boots.

Marcy stroked his head more, her gaze still

locked on me. "We're going to need to have a long discussion about what you are. About what we all are, Dana."

I knew as much but wasn't feeling up for it just yet. "Later?"

She sighed and nodded. "Later works. What are you going to do today after your run? Tell me it involves something that won't leave your fingers raw."

I glanced at my red hands. The skin on my knuckles was the worst. It looked as if I'd gone several rounds with a heavy bag when, in reality, I'd merely tackled scrubbing the old wood floors.

"I have a cream that will help them," she said softly. "If you're open to trying it."

"Did you make it by normal means, or did you say some kind of hocus-pocus over it?" I asked. The question was legit.

She snorted. "I cursed three times while making it because I splashed hot oil on myself. Does that count?"

I laughed. "Depends on what curse words you said. I've heard your version of cussing, and frankly, I've heard eight-year-olds do a better job."

She stared at me, looking to be fighting the urge to outright laugh. "Why am I picturing you at age eight, needing a bar of soap put in your mouth?"

"Probably because you know me well," I added with a smirk. "Burgess seems content."

He had fallen asleep in her arms.

She winked at me. "You like him. Admit it."

"I like him more when he's not in my boots," I returned.

She continued to stroke him lovingly as he napped. "When are you going to head over to see your new offices?"

With everything that had happened since we'd gotten to Grimm Cove, I'd not had a chance to really stop and think about the fact I was taking over the firm of a retiring local attorney. He had offices in a building here in town with other lawyers, and I'd not once even considered going to see what it was I'd gotten myself into. I was almost afraid to look, seeing as how everything else had gone sideways since my arrival in town.

It had been at the forefront of my mind on the way to South Carolina, but the second I found myself face-to-face with a bunch of evil assholes with fangs, I kind of forgot about much else.

Hard to focus on things when you get a hefty dose of reality tossed at you.

"It will get easier," said Marcy.

"What will?" I asked before remembering who I was talking to. The woman was basically a mood ring, wrapped in an oracle, covered in a nice coating of freak-me-out.

"Processing the knowledge there is more to the world than you thought. That there is more to *you* than you'd thought," she said, confirming my assessment of her. "You made short work of a number of the vampires who attacked us. You have to know that isn't something a normal person can do, right?"

I shivered slightly as I thought about how effortlessly I'd killed more than one vampire, and how much I'd taken the death of the succubus-witch-bitch who had tried to kill us in stride.

Marcy nudged me with her elbow. "She had it coming."

"You read minds now too?" I asked, only partially joking, since I wasn't sure she didn't.

"No. I've known you twenty years. I can read your facial expressions and your aura. You have a lot of inner turmoil happening right now," she said matter-of-factly. "You're at odds with what your head has always been told was true about the world, versus what *is* true. Right now, both sides are having a standoff. I've met your grandmother, so I know you come by your stubborn streak honestly."

I did my best to avoid making a witty retort. Mostly because I was trying to be more open-minded about the idea that witches, shifters, vampires, demons, and a whole other slew of supernatural creatures were real.

Ironically, I'd been raised Catholic, and while we believed in demons, the devil, and God, not many of us walked around thinking we'd run into a demon. They were something we'd worry about after death when we went to wherever it was we went. Not something we could bump into at the supermarket.

From what I was learning about Grimm Cove, having a demon at the corner market with you wasn't out of the realm of reason. In fact, if Poppy's brand-spanking-new husband was to be believed, there were several businesses owned and operated by demons in town.

Brett just so happened to be Poppy's high school sweetheart, first love, current husband, and fated mate or something, but I'd not gotten all the details just yet, so I was a bit fuzzy on how all that worked.

I was fuzzy on a lot.

All I knew was that we'd rolled into town forty-eight hours ago, she'd hit the tree outside of Brett's house, and out he came——rushing headfirst back into her life after being gone from it for twenty years. The two wasted no time bumping uglies, and if I dared to believe one of the two ghosts residing with us, Poppy and Brett were now married in the eyes of the supernatural community and expecting twins.

Marcy made a move to head deeper into my room with her pet tree-rat, and I blocked her path. She grunted. "Has anyone ever told you that you're very hostile?"

"People tell me that daily," I said.

She sighed. "Good. I'd hate for you to forget."

"Not likely."

She continued to pet Burgess as she glanced up at me. "You should see if Jeffrey is free today. He could visit your new office with you."

"Jeffrey?" I asked, unsure why Marcy would bring up Brett's best friend.

"Yes," she said, a knowing look on her face. "I'm sure he'd find time in his schedule to take you over there."

"I don't need a male escort," I returned, my thoughts instantly going to the tall, sandy-blond-haired hunk. He, like Brett, was more than met the eye. And just like Brett, he was a wolf-shifter. I hadn't actually seen either of them shift forms yet and wasn't sure I wanted to. But I had to wonder if my imagination was making more out of it than it truly was. Then again, the dude could turn into a freaking wolf, so it's not as if it was no biggie.

"Any reason why you keep turning down Jeffrey's advances?" she asked coyly. "I know he's not like the men you normally date—you know, the ones with designer suits specially tailored for them, watches that cost more than most people make in a year, full of legalese, but he's very attractive and funny."

Very attractive didn't even begin to cover what Jeffrey Farkas was. I'd seen a lot of hot guys in my life, but he took the cake. And Marcy was right, Jeffrey was a far cry from the arrogant city guys I'd played hide the cannoli with in the past. He was rugged and rough around the edges. Oddly, I found that hot as hell.

The guy had a body to die for, but there was something about him that was off-putting. Like how *my* body seemed to react to his each and every time he was around. It was as if I went into heat the minute I heard his voice and had to fight to keep my mind from wandering to the bedroom.

That wasn't like me.

I didn't get swept up in men.

At least I hadn't since I was in my teens, and even that paled in comparison to the way my ovaries stood at attention the second they detected the alpha male in my vicinity.

I wasn't one of those pathetic women who drooled over a man and lost themselves in a guy. I was a serious career woman, and my focus needed to be on coming to grips with the fact supernaturals were real and getting my practice up and running smoothly.

Not on getting Jeffrey into bed.

I just wished my hormones understood as much. They were all for me being a pathetic drooling mess of a woman. They were Team Jeffrey, and they were about as easy to argue with as Nonna.

My hormones had a sexual awakening about two seconds after my introduction to Jeffrey. That had come in the form of me accidentally punching him in the face. From there, we'd spent the greater part of my first day in Grimm Cove practically joined at the hip.

He'd helped with moving us into the house and we exploited his muscles for all they were worth. Just thinking about seeing him lift heavy objects made my insides flutter with anticipation of more.

Didn't hurt that he'd played the hero as well. He'd come charging in during the succu-bitch's attempt to kill us and had helped take out some of her minions. He'd then proceeded to spend the entire day after trying to take me out—on a date, that is.

I'd nearly said yes.

Something deep down had stopped me from accepting his offers. Like maybe saying yes to a date wouldn't end there. That it would lead to something more. Something I wasn't sure I was ready for and had a fairly good idea the playboy wasn't ready for either.

Sure, Nonna would be thrilled, but I couldn't worry about that. I had other things to focus on.

Jeffrey wasn't one of them.

"Thinking about the very sexy wolf-shifter?" asked Marcy with a grin.

I grunted. "No."

"Sure you're not," she mouthed, as she left my room, leaving the door standing wide open. The tree-rat went with her. I counted my blessings where I could get them and went to work locating my other running shoe.

I needed to blow off steam, and quick. It was that or risk a homicidal incident. Or worse yet, risk hunting Jeffrey down and using him to alleviate my hormonal overload.

SIX

Jeffrey

JEFFREY SAT on the edge of Brett's desk, holding a cup of coffee in his hand from Demon Grounds Coffee Café, which was by far his favorite in town. Not that he'd ever confess as much to the owner of Magik Brew. She made a very nice cup of coffee, but her strong suit was tea and other types of drinks.

Brett entered his office, in full uniform, looking official and respectable. He raised a brow as he spotted Jeffrey plopped on the edge of his desk.

Holding up a second cup of Demon Grounds coffee, Jeffrey grinned. "Grabbed you one too."

"Thanks," said Brett, coming for the coffee. He took it and then walked around to the other side of his desk and sat in a large black leather chair. "If you're here, who is handling restocking the bar and overseeing things there?"

"Austin," said Jeffrey.

"Finally letting the guy do the job you're paying him for rather than making him a delivery boy?" asked Brett.

"Something like that."

Brett took a sip of his coffee and went to work keying in something on his keyboard. He had an interesting system of hunting and pecking but at a fast pace. "I'm not going to put in a good word for you with Dana. Stop asking."

"How do you know I'm here for that?" asked Jeffrey.

He *was* there for that, but still.

Brett kept typing. "Because for the last two days, you've tried just about anything you can to convince me to get her to go on a date with you. Face it, buddy, she's just not that into you."

"I find that hard to believe," countered Jeffrey. "Chicks dig me. And women don't turn me down. Ever."

"This one does," said Brett with a shrug. "As much as she possibly can. Speaks highly of her character. Don't ya think?"

"Bro, I brought you coffee," pleaded Jeffrey.

"Your favorite kind. Cut me some slack and set me up on a date with your roomie. Convince her to give me a go."

With a groan, Brett kept typing and staring at his computer screen as he spoke. "She's not my roomie. Poppy and I haven't ironed out the living arrangement yet."

"Meaning you live with your mate, her two besties, her deceased yet hardly gone grandparents, and her adult twins?" asked Jeffrey, holding back his laugh.

"Yeah," said Brett, glancing up from his task briefly. He looked tired at the mention of everyone currently calling the Proctor House home.

"You just got the old Belliveau house all restored. You up for taking on another project? Especially one the size of the Proctor place?" asked Jeffrey, already knowing the answer. Growing up, there had been two homes in Grimm Cove that Brett had always taken a shine to. One was Mrs. Belliveau's home, which he'd purchased and restored after her passing. The other was the Proctor House. There was no way he was going to miss out on a chance to get his hands on the house and restore it as well.

Jeffrey had never been bitten by the remodeling

bug. Sure, he helped Brett often because it gave them time together, and as best friends, it's what you did, but he didn't find a ton of joy in it.

He preferred being at his place near the water. He liked to fish and be out on his boat. That was his happy spot.

"Poppy and I haven't had a chance to discuss me fixing the place up just yet," he said, his typing slowing. "Tuck is all for it."

"Having conversations with her long-dead grandfather has got to be tops on the 'shit I wouldn't have guessed would happen to you' list," said Jeffrey, still amused with Brett's situation.

Better him than me.

Jeffrey was happy to be a free agent. Able to play the field and do who and what he wanted, whenever he wanted to do it. He didn't have anyone to answer to except himself. Brett currently had a laundry list of people to answer to.

"Tuck and I are doing okay," said Brett. "He's happy I'm with his granddaughter now and excited about having more great-grandchildren, but I'm a guy. That means he's not a fan of me having *alone* time with Poppy. If you catch my drift."

"He doesn't want you doing the nasty with his granddaughter. He has a look-but-don't-touch policy." Jeffrey laughed so hard he nearly fell off the side of the desk. "Is Ellie-Sue any better about it?"

"She's pretty much the only reason I've gotten alone time with my wife," admitted Brett. "But I came around the corner yesterday evening, before dinner, to find her pressing Poppy for details on my bedroom skills. She wanted to know if I stacked up against the ex."

"Do you?" asked Jeffrey.

Brett's eyes flashed from chocolate brown to yellow, signaling his wolf was close to surfacing fully. "I can't believe you asked me that."

Lifting his hands while still holding his coffee, Jeffrey did the universal signal for surrender but couldn't help but laugh. "Forget I asked."

After a few tense seconds, Brett's eyes returned to normal.

That was good. Jeffrey really didn't want to pull the alpha card on him. Sometimes it sucked being the top dog.

Brett had spent the greater part of nineteen years watching over Poppy and her children while she was married to another man. A human. One who'd ended up opening the door for a succubus to make a move against Poppy and everyone close to her.

Thankfully, they'd all come out of the other side of the ordeal in one piece. The succubus and the men she'd enthralled into doing her bidding were dead and gone. While they were no longer a threat, Jeffrey couldn't let go of the idea that all was not perfect in the town and something dark lurked right around the corner.

He was probably reading too much into it all.

Waiting for the other shoe to drop was more his father's style than his. Did that mean he was becoming like his dad? It wasn't a thought he wanted to entertain. He'd spent his life living in the man's shadow.

He had to admit he missed the days when there was little to no responsibility to be had.

Jeffrey had spent a chunk of the day prior visiting with the Helens family, offering his condolences on the passing of Robbie. He'd been one of the succu-bitch's victims. The idea that Robbie was dead and gone still hadn't totally sunk in for Jeffrey.

Stella was taking it hard, and that was to be expected. She and Robbie had finally acted on the attraction they'd had for one another. They'd not been a couple long when he'd died.

"Hey, have you seen Ryan around?" asked Jeffrey.

Brett glanced at him, sighed, and shook his head. "No. Travis mentioned hearing Ryan was taking off to the Helenses' hunting cabin to be alone. I don't know how true that is. How is the rest of the family doing?"

"As good as can be expected," said Jeffrey, wishing their world wasn't a violent one. The truth of the matter was, he and Brett tended to process death differently than others. They'd seen a lot of it while in the military and more than their fair share prior to enlisting.

Death was part of the shifter world.

They didn't like it, but they'd learned to accept it—at least for the most part.

"How goes it with the twins? Any trouble in paradise since they rolled into town?" asked Jeffrey, wanting to change the subject. He had to throw himself into a topic that wasn't the loss of a pack mate.

Poppy had a son and a daughter from her first marriage. The children were eighteen now and freshmen in college. They were also in Grimm Cove, having just gotten into town yesterday. Jeffrey had met them briefly when he'd run into them at the market with their mother. While they seemed like very nice, very well-mannered young adults, he had to wonder how they were handling the news their mother had been claimed by a wolf-shifter and was now considered married in the eyes of the supernatural community.

Not to mention, the news supernaturals were a real thing.

Brett stopped working and stared up at Jeffrey. "Oddly, they've been fine with it. Correction, Pepper seems totally fine with it all. Happy for her mother, and me even. Tucker is civil and perfectly respectful, but I think he's not as quick to trust others. Namely me. I think he's worried I'll hurt his mother like his father did. He's got a lot of resentment for Thomas going on. Poppy's tried to talk to him about it, but he's not very receptive. I offered to give it a go, but no one thought that was a good idea when I brought it up."

From what Jeffrey had learned through Brett, Poppy's ex-husband had spent the whole of their nineteen-year marriage having affairs with other women. But Poppy hadn't found out until the end, when he'd informed her that he wanted a divorce and didn't love her anymore. That he was in love with a woman he barely knew.

Karma was a bitch, because the woman he ended up leaving Poppy for turned out to be a succubus-witch hybrid who had only been using the man to gain access to Poppy and the Proctor House.

For as much as that all had to suck for Poppy to go through, it had put her on the same page as Brett once more. And Brett had wasted no time claiming her. Unlike the first time they were a couple. He'd gone and screwed the pooch on that one big time. But Fate had found a way to right the wrongs of the past and Jeffrey couldn't recall a time he'd ever seen Brett happier.

"Mated life suits you, brother," said Jeffrey before taking a drink of his coffee.

A smile touched Brett's lips. "I still can't believe it's real."

"Believe it. In like nine months, you'll have a set of twins to prove it," said Jeffrey with a grin. "Can't wait to see you doing diaper duty."

Brett took a deep breath. "Ellie-Sue told me that Poppy won't go full term with the twins. She'll have them sooner than that."

"How bizarre is it to have conversations with your wife's dead grandmother?" asked Jeffrey.

Brett tipped his head to the side. "It's pretty out there. Tuck and Ellie-Sue just pop up anywhere, at any time. That's gonna take some getting used to."

"I'll bet," said Jeffrey. "Unless you and Poppy decide to move into your house. It's plenty big."

"She'd never leave her family home, and I'd never ask her to," said Brett evenly.

"What about having Marcy and Dana move into your house?" asked Jeffrey. "That would free up space and give you two a little more privacy."

"You want to be the one to bring that up to my wife?" asked Brett.

Jeffrey thought on it. "Nope. Best I can tell you is to see if you can get the ghosts to wear bells or something to announce their arrival."

Chuckling, Brett sat back in his chair and took his coffee with him. "I miss this."

"Coffee?" asked Jeffrey.

"Yes. Dana is the only one at the house who drinks it, and she has some fancy coffee press thing that I can't figure out. I know I look about as country as country can get to Poppy's friends and kids. I don't want to go asking how to work the press and prove just how country I am. I watched a video on the internet but apparently, I'm all thumbs. I made a mess. My only option in the morning has been herbal tea," said Brett, the look on his face speaking volumes.

Unable to help himself, Jeffrey laughed. "Gag."

Brett nodded.

"So, Dana likes coffee, huh?" asked Jeffrey, his mind spinning with ideas to woo her.

Groaning, Brett sat up in the chair once more. "I don't know what you're thinking, but stop. I know you. You're not used to being told no. That means you're going to go above and beyond to get your way. Leave this one alone, Farkas. She's my wife's best friend. You rock that boat and they'll never find your body."

Jeffrey nearly joked it off but stopped, instead fumbling with the plastic lid of his coffee cup. "I'm not sure I *can* leave it alone."

"What do you mean?" asked Brett. "It's easy. Just find another skirt to chase. You're good at that. Ask your momma. She'll tell you all about your skirt-chasing ways."

She would. He was right. But there was something about Dana that felt different from the other women. Sure, she'd turned him down each time he'd asked her out, so there was that, but there was something more. He just couldn't quite pinpoint what that something more was.

A nagging deep inside him kept insisting he try again with her.

"Well?" pressed Brett.

With a shrug, Jeffrey remained silent.

"Shit," breathed out Brett. "Tell me you didn't."

"Didn't what?" asked Jeffrey, turning more on the desk to face Brett better.

His friend's expression was nothing short of astonished. "You went and fell for a woman finally. And the one you decided to go all head over heels for just so happens to be the one woman who has zero issues telling you to go fu—"

"Chief," said Stratton Bright, cutting off Brett as he poked his head into the office. His brown hair was pushed back from his face and gelled in some fancy big-city-boy way, reminding everyone that he'd moved to Grimm Cove from Chicago, and wasn't born there. Brett had hired him on a few years back and given him the position of lead detective. He was always dressed like he might be asked to pose for the cover of a men's magazine.

Jeffrey didn't get it. He preferred jeans and T-shirts to dress slacks and dress shirts. He couldn't imagine Stratton was comfortable done up like that all the time.

Stratton nodded to him but then spoke to Brett. "Charmaine said a call just came in from the Pick-enses' farm."

Brett sighed. "Did she spend an hour talking on the phone asking about the state of things with the cows this year? I swear, our dispatcher spends more time chatting with people than anyone I know."

Stratton shook his head. "No. She wasn't on long. Something about dead farm animals drained of their blood. She didn't catch it all but there may have been partially eaten animals too."

Jeffrey tensed. The first culprit that came to mind was vampires, but they didn't eat things so much as drained them dry.

The vampires in Grimm Cove knew better than to pull a stunt like that. They were already on blast because of the recent succubus attack, when she'd brought vampires with her. Thankfully, none had been local and from what Brett and everyone involved had been able to dig up, all had been evil dicks to start with.

So no big loss to society or anything now that they were extra dead.

"Vampire?" asked Brett of Stratton, clearly thinking the same thing as Jeffrey.

"Doc Hartshorn made the call," said Stratton, his expression serious.

Dr. Donte Hartshorn was a trusted friend and

veterinarian. If he was calling in about an issue concerning animals, there was a problem.

Brett stood. "Head on out and take a look. Call me with what you find."

"Will do," said Stratton, heading out.

Jeffrey stood as well. "You don't think we missed some succubus thrall stragglers, do you?"

"I sure the hell hope not," added Brett. "I've got a couple of things I have to wrap up here that can't wait. Can you stop by the house and check on the girls?"

Jeffrey waggled his brows. "Can do."

Brett grunted. "And avoid lame come-ons to Dana?"

"Probably not," admitted Jeffrey. "Still want me to head over?"

"Unfortunately, yes," he said. "Let me know how they're doing."

Jeffrey eyed his friend, wondering why Brett was passing on the opportunity, no matter what he had going on at work. "You're not going because Poppy forbid you from hovering, right?"

"Um, no," said Brett so quickly, it was easy to see he was lying.

Jeffrey laughed. "I'll go and report in. It's on

my way over to the bar anyways. Plus, gives me a chance to convince Dana to have dinner with me."

"When I get home tonight and find your balls in a jar on the table, I'm not going to be too shocked," said Brett as he walked toward the door to his office.

Jeffrey joined him. "It's fine. My balls will be sitting there next to yours, or have you missed the fact you're scared of your wife's reaction to you checking in on her again? Hell, the women probably pass your balls around and laugh at how fast she jarred them."

"Asshole," muttered Brett.

Jeffrey grinned. "Yep."

Brett slid him a sideways glance. "Wouldn't it be something if it turned out to be alpha ball-canning season?"

Instinctively, Jeffrey reached down and cupped himself protectively.

SEVEN

Dana

I HELD up my right foot behind me, stretching in preparation for my run. Marcy had followed me outside. She had a pitcher with some sort of liquid in it as she walked toward three old hummingbird feeders hanging from a tree. I continued doing my pre-run stretches as I watched her filling the feeders with the liquid.

She seemed content and had her ride-or-die companion with her—Burgess. He was propped on her shoulder, hanging on for dear life to the spaghetti strap of her tank top. I still wasn't a hundred percent sure what a familiar was, but if it wasn't getting hazard pay being with Marcy, it really needed to find a new line of work.

She glanced over her shoulder at me. "Have you had any coffee yet?"

"Not before my run, why?" I asked, pulling my long ponytail tighter.

She glanced at Burgess, raising her brows as she did. "Stay far from her until she's caffeinated."

I rolled my eyes and snorted before moving to stretch my other leg. When I was done, I checked to be sure my cell phone was all set on my armband. My cell was loaded with various playlists I liked to run to. Most of them consisted of '80s music.

A cord around the back of my neck held my Bluetooth earbuds. The cord kept them tied together so in the event one fell out while I was running, it wouldn't just go flying in any old direction. Whenever I needed to take them out while I was running, I could simply let them hang around my neck and shoulders and they remained in place.

No muss.

No fuss.

They'd actually been a gift from Marcy for my fortieth birthday. She'd also gotten me a set of healing crystals. I put them with the deck of tarot cards she'd gotten me the year prior. Those, of course, had been with the rune stones she'd given me the birthday before that, and so on.

All of which remained unopened.

Basically, the earbuds were the most normal thing she'd ever gifted me. Unless, of course, they were some kind of aura-cleansing device that she'd found a way to secretly get me to use. Wouldn't put it past her. She'd probably had them blessed by a shaman or something.

I was about to head out for my run when the sound of country music came filtering down the street from the world's biggest silver pickup truck. I'd seen the truck more than once in the last forty-eight hours and had to admit I was secretly pleased to get a glimpse of its owner.

Marcy laughed. "Look who is coming to no doubt ask you on another date."

Jeffrey had the windows down, and despite the early hour, had his music at a level that would have gotten a few choice words directed at him from New York City folks hanging their heads out their windows.

His sandy-blond hair was just past his ears and was laced with white at the temples. His stubble-covered jaw was a mix of shades of light brown, blond, and white, giving him a rugged appearance.

His blue gaze held nothing but mischief as he pulled into the driveway and put the truck in park.

Marcy waved emphatically in Jeffrey's direction, causing Burgess to nearly topple off her shoulder. The tree-rat grabbed her hair and clung tight.

Jeffrey glanced in her direction, gave a nod and a thousand-watt smile, showing off his dimples, and then paused in his step. His gaze narrowed before he continued heading for the porch, closer to me.

The light breeze blew his scent to me, filling my head with the smell of cardamom and pears. They were smells I knew from helping Nonna in the kitchen, and they oddly reminded me of home, of good days when life was simple, and the trials and tribulations of adulthood had yet to reach me.

Stand strong, Van Helsing, I thought to myself. *You can do this. You can resist his charm.*

He ran a hand through his hair, making the red T-shirt he had on lift slightly, revealing his toned abdomen. There was a dusting of brown hair peeking out, and I had the strongest urge to rush down the porch steps, tackle the man to the ground, yank up his shirt, and see the entire show.

Instead, I went with stretching out my arms. Seemed less likely to get me pregnant.

As his smile widened upon approach, I wasn't so sure about that.

Good God, the man is lick worthy. Way to resist.

"Does she have a squirrel on her shoulder?" he asked, his voice deep, his Southern accent thick.

Was it possible to end up pregnant by sheer proximity to hotness?

He stared at me, and I realized he'd asked a question.

Think, Van Helsing. What did he say?

He smirked. "You all right there?"

"Fine. You?" I asked, the lie falling from my lips with ease.

"Just stopping by to check in on y'all. There was an issue on the outer edge of town and Brett asked me to look in on you three lovely ladies."

I lowered my arm and glanced around to see if anyone else was out and about this time of morning. I didn't see anyone, but I lowered my voice all the same. "Like a normal problem or a paranormal problem?"

He leaned in toward me and bent slightly, putting him nearly nose to nose with me. "Why are you whispering?"

I didn't budge or raise my voice. "I thought the stuff about you guys was a secret."

"What stuff?" he asked.

I found it difficult to focus with how close his lips were and how good the man smelled. Clearly, I had no ability to resist him. It took me longer than it should to realize those sexy lips of his were twitching as he fought to keep from laughing. "The part about you being able to shift into a dog and lick your own butt."

"Anyone else calls me a dog, I get angry," he said, remaining in place. "You do it and I find it hot as hell. Why is that?"

"I don't know. Were you dropped on your head as a child?" I countered.

"Maybe. You want to ask my momma? She's dying to meet you ever since your name came up in conversation yesterday," he said.

My breathing increased as I eased even closer to him—specifically, his lips. "You told your mother about me?"

"You two should really just kiss and get it over with," said Marcy, startling me because I hadn't realized she was standing so close to the porch. She had the hose in one hand and was filling a metal watering can, smiling widely up at Jeffrey and me. "Or you could skip to the good stuff and go to Jeffrey's cabin near the water, get buck naked, and do the deed."

Marcy had never thrown me at a man before. She wasn't Nonna. She didn't spend every waking moment around me trying to convince me to land a Mr. Dana. This was new behavior for her, and honestly, I had to hand it to the girl—she had some great ideas.

He's got so many strings attached to him he could form a ball of yarn.

It was true. He was best friends with my best friend's husband, mate, or whatever the heck you wanted to call Brett. That meant after I got what I wanted from him and was done, he wouldn't go away. He'd always be around, and that would lead to a lot of awkward moments. Plus, the man could turn into a wolf and actually lick his own butt.

"Well, since neither of you has moved a muscle, I'm going to assume you're waiting for me to walk away so you can just get naked and do your business right here," said Marcy as Burgess ran down her arm and leapt at the porch railing.

He made it with ease and skittered by before jumping down to the porch floor and darting in the open front door.

As I watched the tree-rat vanish into the house, I felt the heavy weight of Jeffrey's stare. When I glanced back at him, I found him grinning like the cat who ate the canary.

"What?" I asked.

He winked. "I'm game if you are."

"Game?"

"For getting naked and doing the deed. You in?" he asked. "Say you're in, Legs. The fun we could have."

I opened my mouth and knew without a shadow of a doubt if I didn't do something quick, I was going to take this man to bed. A procession of string attachments was sure to follow. I took the mature, adult way out of the situation. I stuck my tongue out at him and stepped back fast.

His laugh raced over me, making my insides warm.

He inhaled deeply, his royal blue eyes quickly turning icy blue.

My breath caught. It was as if someone had dumped a bucket of ice water over my head, cooling my ardor instantly. While I'd been told more than once he could shift into a wolf and was supernatural, I'd never seen him doing anything close to it. This was new, and I had to admit, it both freaked me out and turned me on.

Reaching out, I touched his cheek, my gaze locked on his. "Holy...what in the...wow."

He blinked several times quickly and stood tall once more, clearing his throat as he did. He ran a hand into the back of his hair, clearly uncomfortable all a sudden with the situation.

I wasn't sure what to do or say so I blurted out the first thing that came to mind. "Run."

He looked confused.

"You run. No, wait. Me. *I'm* running," I said before shaking my head. "I mean I'm going for a run."

Marcy chuckled as she turned off the water. "Hard to believe you are a powerful attorney and make people quake in fear on the stand."

I gave her a stern look before turning to run, only to slam right into Jeffrey who had stepped into my path. The minute we collided, heat poured through me, and I gasped.

So did he, yanking me closer to him.

The next I knew, a low grumble started deep in his chest, turning quickly into a full-blown growl. His eyes flashed to icy blue once again and he jerked me tighter to him, to the point it wasn't exactly comfortable.

Now would be a great time to start resisting. I opened

my mouth to do just that and got another whiff of his scent. Man, he smelled good.

You are weak, Van Helsing.

Gathering my resolve, I pushed on his chest. "Back it up there, buddy."

His eyes returned to normal and he released me.

I was the one who actually backed up, mainly because my head was yelling retreat, but my hormones were shouting at me to charge ahead with thrusters set to do-the-hunk.

Somehow, Marcy had managed to go from being down in the side yard, near the end of the porch, to standing behind us on the porch watering flowers all without my noticing. Since there were too many potted plants to count, it was a task that was time consuming for sure.

I touched my chest, mostly to be sure my heart hadn't actually leapt out of it, and then glanced nervously in her direction for clarity on the situation. Should I run or do the guy?

Shit was getting real when I sought out guidance of someone who spent more time talking about auras than any person ever should.

She was humming a Richard Marx song, moving

her head back and forth as she did. I couldn't fault her music choice but it was painfully clear I wasn't going to be getting any assistance from her.

"I have to run," I said quickly, more to myself than anyone else.

Jeffrey's cock-sure grin reappeared on his handsome face. "You *sure* you want to?"

"Yes," I replied, only to realize I was shaking my head "no" simultaneously. When it came to him, conflicting messages were my running theme. I took a second to compose myself and put my earbuds in. "I'm sure."

He spoke loudly, not that he needed to, seeing as how I hadn't actually started any music. "How about I join you for your run?"

"I need some alone time," I said faster than anyone would ever need to. "And you're in jeans and boots. Not running attire."

Marcy touched my shoulder, startling me in the process. My gaze whipped to her. She smiled. "I think that's a lovely idea. After all, he's from here. Stands to reason he knows the various paths in the woods. Since that's the way you were going, it makes sense to take him along. I think I saw a duffle bag Brett brought over with some gym clothes in it. I'm sure he wouldn't mind if Jeffrey borrowed them."

"I never said I was running in the woods." While I'd not said it, I had been planning on doing just that. Since the woods butted against the property of the house, they'd been calling to me, offering a form of escape from all of the crazy that had become my life over the past forty-eight hours. Right now, it was also an escape from the way Jeffrey made my body react.

"You're planning to head out into the woods alone?" asked Jeffrey, his voice even louder than before.

I removed the earbuds to prevent him from full-out shouting at me. My stubborn streak reared up. "Yes."

"Not happening," he said sternly.

I squared my shoulders. He wasn't trying to tell me what I could and couldn't do, was he? Surely, I'd heard him wrong. "Uh, yeah, it is."

He stiffened. "I said no."

"Oh, you just made sure it's happening."

He snorted but it didn't sound jovial. "Try again, Legs."

I glanced at Marcy to find her looking amused.

"He doesn't honestly think he's going to win this argument, does he?"

She licked her lips, fighting another smile. "I'd say he thinks he stands a better-than-average chance, seeing as how he's the alpha of the pack here. And it's a really big pack, Dana."

I took a moment to think about what she was saying. My gaze narrowed. "He's the guy in charge of the, um, *you know*?"

"The wolf-shifters?" she asked, sounding entirely too pleased with the way the whole talk was going.

I nodded.

"You can say what he is when it's just us," she supplied. "Unless, of course, the idea of what he is freaks you out too much. Is that it?"

"I'm not scared of him because of that," I said, wanting the words back the second they left my mouth. I didn't like the way he made me feel or the massive disconnect he caused between my brain and my body.

"You're scared of me?" asked Jeffrey, some of the fight leaking out of his voice.

I went to push past him, my need to start my run and be done with the conversation and the vulnerability it brought out it in me too great to resist.

Jeffrey caught my hand in his and held it.

The same warmth I'd felt before returned, this time spreading up my arm.

"Dana, you don't have to be scared of me," he said, his voice soft. With how deep his voice normally was, I could only guess that took some work on his part to temper it. "Know that. Please."

I got the sense *please* wasn't a word he said often.

"I do." I gave the slightest of nods and then pulled my hand from his. I was off the porch in record time, putting my earbuds in my ears and heading right for the path that led into the woods. I knew it looked like I was escaping the clutches of the big bad wolf. Since it wasn't too far from the truth, I didn't much care.

"I'm taking you to breakfast when you get back, Legs," he shouted from the porch, just as I started the music, drowning out the rest of whatever he said.

I continued running full-out, secretly pleased I'd be seeing him again in a few hours.

EIGHT

Jeffrey

JEFFREY STOOD ON THE PORCH, near Marcy, watching as Dana ran off into the woods. Every ounce of him wanted to give chase. The wolf in him liked the idea of running after her.

The man kind of did too.

Marcy touched his arm lightly, jerking him from his primal urge to give chase. "Let her be right now. She needs a second to think."

He'd only just met her two days prior, and in the span of forty-eight hours, she'd offered to read his tea leaves, his palm, his fortune, his tarot cards, all while blurting out that his aura was bright red, whatever the hell that meant. She was odd but seemed tender-hearted and harmless.

A bit touched in the head possibly, but sweet all

the same. Poppy was pretty and apparently it was true—like attracted like, because Marcy was as well.

Then there was Dana.

She was smoking hot.

"You said it yourself. She doesn't know the woods or the paths that go through it," said Jeffrey, second-guessing running after her. It was more than easy to get lost in the woods that spanned for hundreds of acres. Even local non-shifters sometimes did. It didn't help that a number of the paths simply stopped being paths the deeper you got. And to the untrained eye, and someone without heightened additional senses like those of a shifter or even a vampire, most of the deep wood areas looked alike. "I should follow her."

Marcy sighed. "Yes and no. Yes, she may get a little turned around out there. After all, she's a city girl whose idea of a run through the woods is running through Central Park. But if you go after her *right this second*, she'll just get mad at you and add to that wall she keeps up around herself."

He'd noticed Dana's tough exterior and had butted up against that very wall more than once in the past forty-eight hours. He got the feeling if he kept doing so, it might become impossible to penetrate. He didn't want that. In fact, that was right up there with him not wanting her to be afraid of him.

Against the wishes of his wolf, he nodded. "You're right."

Marcy patted his arm. "I think I saw some rocking chairs out in the garage. There's a picture inside showing them out on the porch here. If you're not too busy, I'd be eternally grateful if you could carry them out here. They're kind of heavy and I keep meaning to ask Brett to do it but always forget."

"Sure thing," he said, remembering the exact rockers she was talking about.

Tuck and Ellie-Sue's front porch was massive and, back in its heyday held six rockers and three small tables that sat between them. Strategically placed around the rockers and tables were potted flowers, plants, and even some veggies. Potted ferns hung from hooks along the other side of the porch, while flower baskets had hung on the side near the hose. It got more sun so that made sense.

"Thank you," said Marcy, returning to watering plants.

Jeffrey headed off the porch and around the far side of the house to the driveway and then back to the garage. It had swing-open, old-style doors, and there was nothing automatic about them. The padlock had rust on it and wasn't even locked, just hanging there loosely.

He opened the garage and found the rockers and small tables all sitting in a row to the right. He took a rocker in each hand and lifted them high. It didn't matter that they'd been made by Tuck himself years ago and would be considered heavy for a human. To him, they weren't much at all. In no time flat, he had them, as well as the tables, out on the porch where they used to sit. He then began to help Marcy arrange the plants accordingly.

"Tell me she didn't put you to work already this morning," said Poppy as she stepped onto the front porch with a cup of tea in hand.

"Hey, buttercup," said Marcy. "Or should I say sleepyhead."

Poppy blushed. "Sorry. I don't think I've slept that good in years. The kids and Dana are still out cold too. Must be all this fresh air."

Jeffrey went to her and gave her a hug. "Morning. And Dana isn't sleeping. She's out for a run."

Poppy leaned against the doorframe. "Sounds about right. She'd get up at a crazy hour back in New York, go for a run or hit the gym, get cleaned up for the day, do any errands that needed to be done, and still beat everyone into the office."

"She was usually the last to leave the office too," added Marcy.

"I can't believe she gave it all up to come here," said Poppy, sipping her tea. "Want me to make you some breakfast, Jeffrey?"

"Thanks, but I've got plans for breakfast," he said, wanting to hear more about Dana.

She grinned. "How about I make you some tea then?"

His eyes widened. "Uh, no. Thank you though."

She laughed. "Brett prefers coffee too."

"You know your husband can't work her fancy coffee press," said Jeffrey. "But desperately wants a cup of coffee in the morning before work each day. You're in the honeymoon phase still, so he'd never dream of telling you all of this and rocking the boat."

She snorted. "Of course he can't work the press. I told him to bring over anything he wanted from his house. So far, he's brought over some toiletries, his uniform stuff, and a small duffle bag of workout clothing. That's it."

"Sounds like Brett," said Jeffrey. "He's what we like to call a minimalist."

She eyed him. "Does he want to be here, in this house, or would he rather live at his?"

Jeffrey put his hand on her shoulder. "Poppy, he's happy wherever you are. And you know he's always had a thing for this place."

She sighed. "It's kind of crowded. I hadn't realized how much so until I noticed how hard it is to have alone time with him."

"How are the twins doing?" he asked.

"Good. They're taking this all very well, considering. So well, in fact, that they're still out cold. They won't be up for hours yet. They'll sleep through lunch if I let them," she said. "To be young again and be able to hibernate at the drop of a dime."

He smiled. "No judgment from me. I'd sleep past lunch if I could too. Damn adulting keeps getting in the way."

"Doesn't it always?" she countered with a wink. "I'm hoping I can convince Pepper and Tucker to go see Thomas, now that he's in town for who knows how long. He wants to come over here to talk later today, but I'd rather he waits until Brett is home. It's important Thomas see and understand who Brett is to me, and that he will forever be part of my life and our children's lives."

Jeffrey stiffened. "Not sure having Thomas over while Brett is here is a great idea. Why don't we plan that talk when I can be at that meet-up too?"

She glanced up at him. "Because you'll be able to control Brett's wolf side if he gets upset with Thomas?"

"You mean *when* he gets upset with your ex," corrected Jeffrey. "You really want to take a chance and have his wolf get away from him?"

She touched her chin. "We'll wait until you're there too. Good thinking."

"Does he know what Brett is?" asked Jeffrey, wondering just how much the ex knew.

She shook her head. "No. I'm not sure he fully understands what Marla was. How, exactly, do I explain that the woman he ended our marriage for wasn't even human? That she was a cross between a witch and a succubus? And how do I tell him I'm mated to Brett, that Brett can turn into a wolf, and that I'm not only pregnant with Brett's twins, but the children I have with Thomas are witches?"

Jeffrey thought harder on it and shrugged. "Maybe just go with you've moved on and suggest he do so as well. But, um, maybe you should screen who he dates for him. If not, he might end up dating the devil himself."

She laughed until she teared up. "True. I thought about lying to him, but he spent so long lying to me in our marriage that I know what it feels like. I don't think turnabout is fair play. He helped to create Pepper and Tucker. Without him, I wouldn't have them. He has the right to know that magik is real and his children possess it. Besides, I don't think he's planning to leave Grimm Cove anytime soon, so he's bound to catch on eventually. He may have been a crap husband, but he was a good father, and he's a very smart man."

"If you say so," added Jeffrey. "After all, he let you slip through his fingers. Seems like a total dumbass if you ask me."

She snorted.

He lifted his chin slightly. "Tuck and Ellie-Sue up and about?"

As a wolf-shifter, Jeffrey should have been more open-minded about spirits, but they weren't something he'd encountered a lot. When he'd seen Tuck again, it had been jarring to say the least, and a comment the man had made while they'd been battling the succu-bitch had stuck with him.

Tuck had said the succu-witch couldn't

enthrall Jeffrey, Brett, or Travis, who had all been in the area during the attack, because they'd already met their mates. Jeffrey wanted to talk more with him about it at some point, but he didn't want to make a fuss. Besides, he'd probably misheard him.

"I haven't seen them since just after dinner last night. They mentioned they had some things to attend to and something about an old friend of Grandma's they were going on a small trip with, and that was that." She exhaled slowly. "It's so weird having them back—if you know what I mean."

Jeffrey laughed. "I'm sure it is. But I bet it's nice too."

"It is. Want me to make you some coffee? I can work Dana's fancy coffee press," said Poppy with a smile. "I'm who got it for her."

"Thank you but I'm good." He really wanted to know more about the woman who'd occupied his thoughts for the last two days, and Poppy was the perfect person to ask. "So Dana...sounds like she was a powerful attorney up in New York City."

"She was the assistant district attorney," returned Poppy. "That was a huge job. Something she'd worked all of her adult life for. And I'm pretty sure she'd have been top dog in a year or so if she'd stayed on."

He hadn't realized just how much she'd walked away from, and he wondered if she'd go back. It wasn't as if Grimm Cove had anything that impressive to offer her. So far, all the town had done was reveal supernaturals were real and left her fighting off vampires and crazed succu-witches. Not really selling points. Certainly wasn't something they'd be putting on the brochures or anything.

"Did she leave because of burnout?" he asked.

"I'm not exactly sure why she left," said Poppy. "Part of me wonders if she did it because of her worry for me and for Marcy. She doesn't like to admit how much she cares or how big her heart is, but she's always been protective of us."

"Yes, she has," added Marcy. "And making sure we were safe here and okay was part of the reason she came. Another was Nonna Wilma."

"Her grandmother?" asked Poppy. "I thought leaving Wilma alone up there would be one of the reasons she'd have stayed—or why she may go back."

Jeffrey stiffened. "You think she'll leave and go back to New York?"

"I honestly don't know," admitted Poppy. "After

what happened the other night, I wouldn't blame her. I didn't know it would be like this here."

"Sounds like you want to leave too," said Jeffrey. He didn't want to see Brett leave but knew he would if his mate wanted to go.

"No. I love it here. Warts and all." She smiled. "Though I'll admit certain aspects of it will take some getting used to. Like having my dead grandparents around."

Marcy held the watering can to her as if hugging the thing. "Dana loves it here too. She doesn't realize how much she loves it here yet, but she does. She and Tuck get along great. Similar personalities."

"But Grimm Cove isn't home to her," said Poppy. "I was born here and spent my summers here until college. You were born here too, Marcy. But not Dana. What family she has left is up there. I'd try to talk Wilma into coming here to live but I'd need to find a way to explain the supernatural to her."

"Or not," said Marcy as she headed down the stairs and then in the direction of the hose.

Poppy simply shook her head at her friend then focused on Jeffrey. "You sure I can't fix you something to eat?"

He patted his nonexistent gut. "I promise. I'm well fed."

"Yes, but you forget that I now live with your best friend. He eats like he might never see food again," she said, her eyes widening. "I don't know where he puts it all."

"Shifters burn a lot of calories even sitting still."

"I need that diet plan," she said.

She didn't. She looked great. Healthier than when they had been teens, all of them having been nothing more than arms and legs. She'd filled out nicely, not that he'd ever admit as much to Brett. He liked his teeth still located in his head. "So, about Dana?"

Poppy narrowed her gaze on him. "You like her, don't you?"

He shrugged, trying to play it cool. "She's all right."

The look on Poppy's face said she wasn't buying what he was selling. "Just all right?"

With a slight grin, he glanced at the floorboards of the porch. "Better than all right."

"I see." She licked her lips. "So Brett was telling me the truth when he said you've asked her out more than once in the last two days?"

Nervous, Jeffrey ran a hand over the back of his neck. "I did."

"And her response was…?"

He gave her a knowing look. "Guess."

Marcy finished filling the watering jug and headed their way again. "She didn't tell him to eat crap and drop dead—but you know, in Dana's words. Not my cleaner version."

Poppy's smile widened. "Good."

"Uh, she's told me no every single time I've asked her out," said Jeffrey, not following.

"But she hasn't told you to go pleasure yourself, or what Marcy said?"

He looked between the women. "Do the two of you moonlight as preschool teachers? It's like you're scared of saying a bad word."

"Oh, I've dropped my fair share," said Poppy. "Now, answer my question."

He thought about each time Dana had turned him down. "No. I haven't been directed to do either of those things—*yet*. I'm sure it's coming."

"Don't count on it," said Marcy.

Poppy sipped her tea and stared at him for the longest time before motioning to the rocking chairs. "That your doing?"

He nodded.

"Have a seat," she said, going to one and sitting down.

Jeffrey sat in the rocker closest to hers. He leaned forward in it, his elbows going to just above his knees. "Are you trying to tell me it's a good thing Dana has turned me down?"

"Yes," they responded in unison.

"I'm so lost." And he was.

Poppy winked. "Jeffrey, had Dana told you yes right away, it would have meant she just wanted to sleep with you and be done with you."

While that was something he'd normally jump at the chance to have—seeing as how it was his usual modus operandi—the idea of only having one night with her didn't sit right with him. As he thought harder on it, he tensed. "That something she does a lot?"

"I'm guessing no more or less than you do," she returned, sipping her tea as she stared at him above the lip of her cup. "Or are you forgetting your best friend is my mate? Think he hasn't mentioned how you are with women? You'd already showed many shades of that behavior back when we were teens. It didn't surprise me in the least to hear you'd gotten worse."

"You sound like my momma."

She snorted. "Good. I've always liked her."

Jeffrey swallowed hard, suddenly embarrassed by his bed-hopping ways. "This, with Dana, is different."

"I know," she said.

"How?" he asked.

She licked her lips. "Because you're here at sunrise, doing manual labor and trying to pry as much information as you can out of me about one of my best friends. Plus, you keep asking her out despite being shot down more than once."

"Maybe I just like the thrill of the chase," he countered, wanting to save face.

Marcy came close and began watering the plant nearest him. "It's cute that you'd think we'd believe that's all it is. Men are adorable. Simple. But adorable creatures."

He groaned.

The women laughed.

"I should be going now," he said, wanting to be out of their line of fire. He'd come back in a bit to grab Dana for breakfast.

"So soon?" asked Poppy. "However will you be able to give my husband a full report on me if you don't stay longer?"

He froze.

She laughed. "Did Brett send you in his stead because he knows I'm tired of him checking in on me nonstop?"

"I should lie and say no, right?" asked Jeffrey with a laugh.

"If you want me to avoid killing him," she returned.

"Then no. He totally *did not* send me to check in on you," said Jeffrey, sitting back in the rocking chair.

"Uh-huh," she mouthed before laughing. "He'd lie and you'd swear to it. You two are partners in crime."

"Guilty as charged." Jeffrey grinned and tried to be stealthy as he checked his watch to see how long it had been since Dana had left on her run.

The squirrel came running out of the open front door. It leaped up, caught hold of Marcy's skirt, and then looked a lot like Spider-Man as it hurried up her body to her shoulder.

Jeffrey shot Poppy a questioning look.

"Her familiar," said Poppy.

"Is a squirrel?" asked Jeffrey, understanding what a familiar was because of his time around Maria and the council. Hers was a chubby orange cat named Slim. It often accompanied her to Elder meetings, sitting on her lap, giving all the wolf-shifters a sideways glare throughout the entire event.

Poppy nodded. "Mine is a wolf. Go figure."

"Dana's is too," said Marcy, still hard at work watering the seemingly endless potted plants on the porch.

NINE

Dana

————————

MY EARBUDS PUMPED '80s music out with a gusto that matched my mood as I ran deeper into the woods adjacent to the Proctor House property. When I'd started my run—all right, when I'd fled the temptation known as Jeffrey—it had been on a fairly well-established path. At some point that had changed without me noticing. Now I was basically off-path but was enjoying my run too much to stop now. It was cathartic and much needed for my sanity.

The music playing through my earbuds only served to drive me onward. The song choice was one that others wouldn't peg me for. After all, I wasn't known to stand around waiting for any man to save me, let alone hold out for a hero. But the song was one I'd always liked.

I increased my pace, already hearing the sound of my heartbeat in my ears over the sounds of Bonnie Tyler belting out her hero anthem. I wasn't tired and it wasn't a strain. It felt good to let go. Good to expel the energy I'd had building over the past forty-eight hours.

Not to mention the sexual frustration and confusion I had for one hunky alpha wolf-shifter.

"Just run," I said, needing to keep from slipping back into it all in my head. Right now, my head was a scarier place to be than the supernatural hot spot of Grimm Cove. It was as if the town had stepped out of the mind of Tim Burton. It was paranormal themed. From the Hell Fire Charity Event that apparently benefited the fire department, to the Poe Day festivities planned for the coming days and weeks, it was hopping with strange and unusual.

As I ran deeper into the woods, I found the ground to be damp because it clearly did not get the same amount of sunlight the outer portions received due to the canopy of leaves and the density of the trees. Old leaves covered the forest floor, which I suspected boasted many layers. It was an interesting mix of dead leaves that were varying shades of yellow, orange, and brown combined with the new growth of late spring.

The entire area was beautiful and had a draw to it that left me wanting to dive headfirst into its depths even more. It didn't matter that I more than likely wouldn't find my way back to the house with any sort of ease. There was a pull that I couldn't deny, so I didn't bother trying.

A dark blur of movement off to my right caught my attention, and I slowed my pace slightly, going on high alert. My first thought was a horde of evil vampires had found me and wanted to go another round, despite the first ending in a lot of piles of ash. Then I thought about the information on supernaturals I'd gotten from my long talks with Tuck Proctor. He'd told me that vampires couldn't be out in the sun.

Seeing as how I'd waited to start my morning run until the sun came up, the odds of whatever was out here with me being a vampire were slim. That being said, I was still going to be cautious because I was incredibly new to the world of supernaturals and wasn't sure what else might be real.

For all I knew, trees could come to life like in

The Wizard of Oz, get pissy with me, and throw apples at my head.

Hey, it happened to Dorothy.

If Marcy had been with me, she'd have been able to tell me if the trees were on my side or not.

I slowed more when I caught sight of the dark blur again.

When I became very aware that it wasn't a play of light, I came to a full stop. I removed my earbuds, put the strap behind my neck, and stared hard at the area where I was positive I'd seen something large moving. My heart was pounding from all the running and fear. Instinctively, I glanced around my immediate surroundings for anything that could be used as a weapon.

Unless wet leaves were effective in self-defense, I was hosed.

Just then, a huge black wolf stepped out from behind a cluster of trees.

My first instinct was to run far and fast.

As a girl from the city, I wasn't used to wolves running wild or strolling around the woods.

Rats, possibly.

Wolves, nope.

Of course, there was the one time our neighborhood had a huge-ass dog that looked a lot like a wolf. The thing was rabid, and it led to panic, fliers with warnings about it everywhere, and, in the end, a showdown between my mother and the beast.

Standing in the middle of the woods, so deep in them that the sunlight was having issues reaching me, facing down a huge wolf, was a far cry from a city alley and a stray dog with anger issues.

Everything in me screamed that the animal would see me as prey and chase me if I ran. I'd once heard someone mention making a lot of noise when encountering a predator in the wild, but a part of me thought that might not apply to wolves. Maybe it was for bears? How different were wild bears and wolves? I really didn't know because I never made a habit of being out in the wild.

The wolf's eyes caused me to take pause. It had one green eye and one brown. Instantly it made me think of the guy I'd dated in high school, the one who had broken my heart. His eyes had been the same.

Its gaze remained locked on me and it took a few steps in my direction, slowly. I wasn't sure how I felt about that. Was it toying with me? Sizing me up for lunch?

Did wolves travel alone or in packs? If it wasn't

alone, was it keeping my attention on it while its buddies surrounded me for the attack?

My mind raced with a thousand ways this was going to result in my demise before I remembered facing down vampires only two days prior. I'd come out of the other side of that in one piece. That had to count for something. Did it make me the Wolf-Whisperer?

No.

But it did mean I wasn't helpless.

So long as the wolf was scared of leaves being thrown at it, because I really wasn't so sure my sudden action-movie fighting skills were always going to be there or if they'd been a once-and-done thing.

The wolf lowered its head slightly—and a strange sense of being safe found its way to me. I tipped my head. Was it someone I knew?

Jeffrey's eyes had turned to an icy blue back at the house, so I didn't think the wolf was him. I only knew two others. Brett and Travis.

I'd not seen Travis since the night of the attack and couldn't remember his eye color.

"Um, do I know you?"

It nodded.

A big sign it was a shifter, not a normal wolf.

"Travis?"

It just stared at me.

"Brett?"

Was the wolf him in shifted form? I'd seen him in full uniform, prior to him heading out for work earlier in the morning. He'd been standing in the kitchen, in front of my coffee press, looking incredibly befuddled.

I'd said my version of a morning hello, which was a head nod, he'd given one in return, and it felt like we'd had a great conversation.

Then he'd headed out for work for the day.

Did being the chief of police in town mean he could take breaks to shift forms and run through the woods?

Was the wolf before me another of his friends —or pack mates, as he'd told me they were called?

I'd met a slew of them the night of the vampire attack, along with a lot of men whom I'd heard others calling slayers, but I couldn't recall most of their names. I also couldn't remember who among them had one green and one brown eye. Then again, I'd watched Brett's eyes shift from chocolate brown to yellow, so maybe the shades of the wolf's had nothing to do with the person's human eye color.

And maybe the wolf wasn't a shifter at all, but a real one.

A wild one who just so happened to nod when I spoke.

Did South Carolina have those? Probably something I should have considered prior to rushing off into the woods on my own. Dammit. Marcy had been right. I really should have read about the wildlife in the area. If I made it out of this alive, I'd be sure to read the brochures she'd put on my dresser.

Okay, "read" is a strong promise. I'll peruse them.

With a quick glance upward, I moved my hand to the silver cross around my neck and realized that was a bald-faced lie.

Fine. I'll at least pull them out of the boxes I planned to recycle.

I swallowed hard. "Nice puppy. No eating me, okay?"

When the wolf gave a slight nod of its head once again, I realized very quickly it probably wasn't a wild one. It was a shifter.

Oddly, I found the idea the wolf was a shifter comforting. That went to show just how wacky and weird my last few days had been.

I took a seat and let my guard down slightly.

The fact the wolf was male did not go unnoticed. It was hard to miss *just how male* the thing was. I felt downright dirty and wrong for seeing everything the wolf had to offer, so I forced my gaze to its face. As it cocked its head to the side, making one ear flop funny, I couldn't help but laugh.

"Let me guess, Brett have you watching over me while I run?"

He was kind of known for doing stuff like that.

The wolf, thankfully, didn't answer. Had it, I'm not sure I'd have held myself together. It was enough to know the wolf could shape-shift into a man. I didn't want to find out they could talk in wolf form or anything.

"As great and as one-sided as this conversation has been, I'm going to finish my run, all without you eating me," I said before glancing around. "Assuming I can find my way back to the house."

Something rustled in the leaves behind me, and the wolf's demeanor changed. It went from appearing friendly and nonthreatening to rabid in a split second. My gut said the growl wasn't directed at me.

Spinning around, I expected to find a legion of demons or something nefarious. There was nothing there.

When I turned back to face the wolf, it too was gone.

For a moment, I wondered if I'd imagined the entire ordeal. The wolf and everything. It was then the sounds of growling came from farther into the woods, where the sunlight wasn't piercing through the treetops above.

"Go after the wolf-man thing to be sure he's okay, or run like crazy in the opposite direction of the possible legion of demons?" I pondered out loud, as if I was expecting someone to answer.

The growling intensified, and then there was a yip that caused my nerves to become steel. The wolf needed help.

I charged at the darkness. *At* the growling, armed only with my wit and Richard Marx, who I could faintly hear coming out of my earbuds from around my neck.

When it felt as if day had turned to night, I began to second-guess my bravado, but I didn't retreat. I walked into the woods more, my pace slow because undergrowth made running full-out difficult. Not to mention I was having a little trouble seeing the floor of the forest.

As I lifted my hand out in front of me, I realized the darkness was so dense in this section of the woods that seeing in it was becoming troublesome. A sinking feeling came over me because the level of darkness wasn't natural. That could only mean one thing.

It was supernatural.

I stared up again and put my arms out wide. "Oh, come on, man! You have *gotta* be kidding me. Don't you people have some sort of double-jeopardy rule in effect? I already had a run-in with evil thrall-heads, the wolf here, and a succu-bitch this week. I don't need to be swallowed by a shadow monster next!"

When I finished shouting at whoever and whatever might be listening, I let out a long, slow, incensed breath. I could panic. In fact, that sounded like a great idea, but it wasn't as if it was going to do any good.

Nope.

I pulled my cell from my armband to dial Poppy's number. It wouldn't hurt to have someone know where to find my body later after I was eaten by a shadow monster.

I went to call her, only to find I had no bars for service this deep into the woods.

Something moved in the leaves not far from me, and the already low-lit area began to darken rapidly. Quickly, I went to turn on the flashlight option on my mobile phone, only to drop it. I bent fast to retrieve it, thankful it landed with the screen side up because it was backlit and currently showed Richard Marx on one of his album covers. It was the very same song Marcy had been humming earlier.

Ironically, the song that was playing was titled "Should've Known Better."

Richard was mocking me from the '80s. Worse yet, he was right. I should have known better than to chase after a random wolf in the middle of the woods. I just hoped I lived to pass on the life lesson.

TEN

Jeffrey

_____

SURPRISE LIT on Poppy's face at Marcy's comment about Dana having a familiar, but she didn't comment further. Instead, she rocked in her chair.

Jeffrey locked gazes with Marcy. "Dana is a witch?"

He'd seen her hold hands with Poppy and Marcy the night of the succu-bitch attack. Some serious magik had risen and helped to end the enemy. Jeffrey had assumed that magik had come from Poppy and Marcy—that Dana was merely there as a show of support and one heck of a good fighter, seeing as how she'd taken out several vampires all on her own. He'd never given any thought to her being a witch.

For some reason, the label didn't feel right. It felt as if something was missing.

"Part. Small part but a part all the same," said Marcy as if it were no big deal. "She's more than just a witch though."

Poppy looked to be all ears now as well. "W-what do you mean?"

Marcy took a deep breath and appeared to be debating on saying more.

"If you know something, Marcy, please share it," said Poppy.

"*I* don't know," returned Marcy quickly. "I just kind of overhear certain details. The other side whispers about her. So do the trees."

Jeffrey held his tongue. Yep. That woman only had one oar in the water.

"What do they whisper?" asked Poppy.

Marcy frowned. "They talk of betrayal. Darkness. A lot about her father's side of the family and her father."

"He's been dead since she was a baby," countered Poppy. "Are you sure you're communing with the wildlife properly? Seems weird they'd bring him up now."

"Unless he's haunting your house along with

Tuck and Ellie-Sue," said Jeffrey, in an attempt to be funny.

Poppy's eyes widened. "Is he?"

Marcy laughed. "No. He's not one of the other spirits here."

Poppy stopped rocking in the chair. "There are others here? Besides Grandpa and Grandma?"

"Oh yes. It's a way station for spirits. The power the house and the grounds hold attracts them like moths to a flame. Most are harmless. Some aren't. But that's not for you to worry about," said Marcy, sounding totally sane while talking about ghosts. "I will say it can get very noisy at night though with them all shouting at the foot of my bed."

"I'd say ones that aren't harmless are something everyone should be concerned with," said Jeffrey.

Poppy pointed at him. "What he said."

Marcy waved a hand dismissively. "Pish-posh."

"Are you going to tell us what the trees and spirits whisper about Dana?" asked Poppy.

Marcy shook her head. "No. I think it's best we let it play out on its own. Besides, I could be hearing them wrong. It happens sometimes."

Just then, Marcy headed to refill the watering can again. She began to hum as well. It took him a second to realize what the song was and when he did, he caught Poppy's gaze with his own.

"Is she humming a Richard Marx song?" he asked.

Poppy inclined her head. "You get used to it. She's on a kick for him this week. Last month, it was John Denver. The month before it was Hall and Oates. It was Wham! before that. I love Wham!. Wish she'd have stuck with George Michael. Though Blondie wasn't bad. You get the picture."

He chuckled. "I do."

"At least she's on Richard Marx now. Dana likes him. A lot. When Marcy went through her Steely Dan phase, I thought Dana was going to throttle her," added Poppy. "Word to the wise, if you have any Steely Dan on your playlist, consider skipping it if she's around."

"Women are very strange," said Jeffrey.

Poppy winked. "We know."

He grinned.

She glanced in the direction of the woods. "I wish I could have talked to Dana before she headed out. I'm worried about her and how she's handling everything."

He stiffened. "Can I help with anything?"

Poppy looked to him, offering a tender smile. "Thank you, but Dana doesn't accept help with ease. Marcy and I know how to thrust it on her in a way she'll resist less, but having a man offer, well, I'm not sure how it would go over. Besides, I don't think there is anything you could do unless you like to clean."

Confused, he lifted a brow.

"She cleans when she's upset, or when her anxiety levels are high. It's how she channels that excess energy. She darn near scrubbed the finish out of the bathtubs. The floors in this house look new. And I caught her on her hands and knees with an old toothbrush, cleaning the baseboards late last night." Poppy expelled a long breath.

"Everyone processes things differently," he said, trying to set her mind at ease about her friend. It was clear she cared for Dana greatly.

She nodded, appearing far off in thought for a moment. "In college, her mother passed away. She never cried—at least not that we saw—but our place was so clean you could have eaten off the floor. Then, her grandmother insisted on moving out of the apartment that she, her mother, and her grandmother used to share, so Dana threw herself into the task. Organizing everything.

Cleaning the old apartment and scrubbing the new one."

"Her grandmother has come up in conversation more than once in the last couple of days. They're close then?" he asked, hanging on Poppy's every word about Dana.

"They are. Wilma—or Nonna, as Dana calls her—is something else. She's a firecracker," confessed Poppy. "She gives Dana a hard time about never settling down and getting married. Dana thinks it's because of her grandmother's age and how things were done back in Wilma's day."

Jeffrey put his hands on his knees as he nodded once more. "She mentioned the woman is ninety. That makes sense."

"It does but I don't think that's the reason Wilma does it," added Poppy. "I think Wilma's afraid of Dana being alone when she's gone. She's the only family Dana has left because her father died when she was little. Wilma wants to see Dana have someone special. Someone to love and who loves her."

Jeffrey tried to play it cool, not wanting to tip off Poppy on just how interested in Dana he was. "So, she's not like dating anyone or anything?

There isn't some guy she left back in New York or something?"

She scoffed. "Uh, no. Dana doesn't date. She just sort of sees a guy she likes, takes him home for a night and then never speaks to him again. It's why we said it's a good thing she didn't tell you yes right away. And the fact she didn't tell you to pound salt means there is a lot of hope."

"You think?" he asked, wishing that were true.

Poppy leaned back in her rocker more. "You're very different from the men I've seen her gravitate toward."

The wind went out of his sails. "Because I didn't go to a fancy college? The military wasn't glamorous but I'm proud of my time serving. I learned a lot during it all."

"I don't mean it that way. I mean you're not shallow like those men," said Poppy. "You try to hide it, but you have a heart of gold and would do anything for a friend or a loved one. And I know how you are with the ladies, Jeffrey. Women fall all over you."

"*You* never did," he said with a smile. "Then again, you're not my mate, and let the record state I'm damn happy you didn't notice me like that. Brett would have killed me."

She laughed.

He hadn't been joking. Brett would have given him a run for his money.

"So, she dates shallow guys who aren't good with the ladies?" he asked, wanting to know more about Dana.

"Oh, I'm sure they're great with the ladies. But you're different," she said. "I'm not sure how to explain."

"If you figure it out, can you tell me? Because I've asked her out more than once, but she keeps telling me no," added Jeffrey. "Not really used to that."

"I suspect you're not," said Poppy.

Another thought occurred to him. "Is she telling me no because of what I am? Because I'm a shifter?"

Poppy shook her head. "She won't come right out and say she's having trouble processing the fact supernaturals are a thing. It's not her style. But she'll be power washing the house before we know it. If you have a closet or anything you need organized, now would be the time to mention it to her."

He sighed. "Do you think she's scared of me? Of Brett?"

"No," said Poppy sincerely.

Jeffrey lowered his gaze, shame filling him. "I lost control around her this morning. My eyes shifted colors. I think it startled her. I told her she never had to fear me. Ever. But I'm not sure she believes me. If my eyes changing freaked her out, seeing me change all the way would do her in."

"Brett offered to shift for the three of us so we could see what it looked like, but I wasn't sure it was a great idea just yet."

"Because you're worried about Dana or because you're not sure you can handle seeing it?" he asked. They'd been friends since they were teens, and he didn't feel the need to tiptoe around the point with her.

"Both," she said softly, her hand going to her abdomen.

"Poppy, you do understand you're giving birth to babies, not a litter of puppies, right?" he asked, only partially joking.

Relief shone on her face. "Ohmygod, thank you. I didn't want to flat-out ask Brett how that worked, but it was freaking me out."

Unable to help himself, Jeffrey laughed. "You should feel free to ask him this stuff. He won't take offense. If you're worried about something and don't want to ask him, you can always ask his mom or my mom. You know they both adore you. His mother is over the moon about being a grandmother. She'd answer any questions you have."

"Will the babies be able to shift right away?" she asked, paling slightly.

Jeffrey had to fight to keep from laughing at her again. It was clear she'd been obsessing over it all for two days but had been keeping the concern to herself. "No. That won't happen until puberty. Since you're having a girl and a boy, you should be aware that sometimes the females of our species can't fully shift. It's not unheard of. My mom is like that. Her eyes shift colors when she's worked up but beyond that, she doesn't shift forms. Brett's mom does. Stella, who works at my bar, she can do some partial shifts but not a full one. But the boys can shift fully. Then again, I'm not aware of any shifters who are half witch and half shifter. So take that as you may."

She nodded and exhaled slowly. "So I'm not giving birth to wolf pups and I won't walk into the nursery to find puppies in place of my babies?"

"Correct," said Jeffrey, grinning from ear to ear. "You do realize I'm honor-bound to tell Brett about this conversation."

"You are not. You only want to tell him to mock me," said Poppy with a snort.

"Okay, that one, but still," added Jeffrey.

She chuckled more.

Jeffrey checked his watch. "Dana has been gone for a while now. How long does she normally run?"

Marcy answered. "This is longer than normal."

"You don't think she got lost, do you?" asked Poppy, alarm in her voice. "She's a city girl. I'm not sure she's actually ever been in woods before. She's probably wandering around, incredibly angry with nature and the world right now."

"I'm not sure how that is different from any other day," said Marcy as she reached up, took the squirrel from her shoulder, brought it to her lips, and kissed its head. "She's surly daily."

Jeffrey shared his body with an animal, and seeing her kissing a squirrel was still too much for him. He'd have commented but concern for Dana pulled his focus back to Poppy. "I'll go look for her. I'm sure she's fine but to be sure, I can find her. Won't take me long. I can follow her scent."

"See, you *will* be joining her on her run after all," said Marcy, walking past Poppy on her way to the front door.

A bluebird landed on the railing of the porch

and chirped loudly, interrupting the conversation in a rather blatant manner. It proceeded to walk back and forth on the rail, moving its head more like a chicken than anything else. For a split second, Jeffrey could have sworn it sounded like it was whistling the same song Marcy had been humming moments prior. The entire scene was surreal, and Jeffrey found himself glancing at Poppy to see if she thought it was weird as well.

"Is it me or is it trying to tell us something?" asked Poppy, laughing slightly. "And is it doing it to the melody of…no way."

"Oh, he *is* trying to tell us something," said Marcy, lifting a hand to shush Poppy. She then concentrated on the bird. "I'm listening. Go ahead."

Jeffrey would have laughed at the idea Marcy could communicate with birds but at this point, he'd believe anything.

Marcy sucked in a big breath, hurrying to Jeffrey as she did. She grabbed for his hand, clutching it tightly. "I didn't know. If I had known, I wouldn't have let her go out on a run this morning without you from the start."

"What didn't you know?" asked Poppy, her voice barely there. Worry radiated from her, so much so that Jeffrey didn't even need his shifter senses to pick up on it.

Marcy kept hold of Jeffrey's hand, her blue eyes growing moist as the bird continued to chirp and then whistle. "The dead farm animals?"

Jeffrey instantly thought of Stratton entering Brett's office to tell him about dead farm animals drained of their blood out at the Pickenses' farm.

"I'm not following," said Poppy.

Marcy stared straight at Jeffrey. "It's out there in the woods."

"What is?" asked Poppy, stealing Jeffrey's question.

"Something dark and deadly," whispered Marcy. "It's not alone. It brought backup. It's been surviving off farm animals, trying to go unnoticed, but they can't sustain the thing…or what it's brought with it."

Jeffrey's inner wolf felt as if it might burst free of him and become its own entity. It wanted out and to track down Dana that badly.

Marcy frowned. "Rogelio says Dana went way off the path. That she's deep in this thing's hunting grounds. I can't sense what he's trying to convey any more than that because it's too frantic. Something about the smell of death and destruction."

"Rogelio?" asked Poppy.

Marcy nodded to the bluebird. "That's him. I'm getting impressions of darkness, danger, death. And weirdly, impressions of rotten eggs. I don't know what it all means. I just know it's not good."

"Call Brett," he said to Poppy. "Tell him everything. Let him know I'm tracking Dana. Have him alert the pack to trouble."

Marcy teared up. "She should be okay. Probably. Right?"

Jeffrey didn't wait to hear any more. If she was crazy, there was nothing to worry about. He'd find Dana to be sure she wasn't lost. If Marcy wasn't crazy and could talk to animals, then Dana was in danger.

Jeffrey took off running but not from the steps. No. He ran right *at* the side railing, leaped over it, landed with ease in the side yard, and took off for the path into the woods.

He knew Dana's scent, having committed it to memory two days ago when he'd walked into the Proctor House with Brett to find a tall, raven-haired beauty standing next to Poppy—her back to him. He'd been captivated by her from the word go, visually tracing his way over her backside, imagining what it would be like to hold her hips while he drove into her again and again.

Her scent, which was a cross between mint and citrus, had sent his body into a weird reactionary state that left him torn between grabbing her and kissing her and being frozen in place.

He'd gone with frozen in place.

Then she'd hit him right in the face, breaking his stupor.

From that point forward, she'd consumed his every thought. He'd tried to play it cool around her, helping her to move things from the storage pods to the home. But when he'd learned of the attack on the house, on the women there, he'd shut off.

Like now, his sole concern had been her.

Getting to her.

Protecting her.

The thought didn't freak him out. No. It felt right, and it drove him onward as he ran, tapping into the wolf within, letting it up enough to increase his speed even more. He raced through the woods, tracking her scent, veering off the path as he did.

ELEVEN

Dana

I HELD my phone in my hand, staring around the darkness, using the flashlight mode in an attempt to see. It was useless: the dark wasn't normal and didn't seem to give two figs about my pathetic phone light.

I gulped, my free hand going to the cross necklace I wore. "Uh, big evil blackhole thingie, knock it off before I…" I struggled for a good threat. "…um, I have the power of Christ compel you away?"

Nothing happened.

I groaned and looked upward. "Way to have my back there, Big Guy."

Growling came from my right, and it sounded like the black wolf. I rushed in the direction because I was already fully committed to the stupid plan. Seemed noble to try to save the wolf if I could.

That or die with him.

At first, I stumbled over branches and ran into a tree because I couldn't see a thing. An expletive so over the top that anyone from my old neighborhood might have blushed hearing it, flew out of my mouth.

I righted myself and took a moment to try to get my bearings. Whatever was out there with the wolf and me had other things in mind. Not only did the darkness totally cut off my ability to even see my phone, which was still in my hand, it felt oppressive, like the longer I was in it, the less likely I was to get out.

Something brushed against my leg, and I nearly lashed out. My gut said not to, and I listened. I did, however, reach down, coming into contact with fur. Relief spread through me. "Wolf dude?"

It nudged me hard enough to make me back up. The wolf then planted itself before me, growling at something I couldn't see or hear.

I patted its hind end and coughed a bit. "Good boy, but no dying on my account. How about we just leave the darkness to itself and get the hell out of here?"

The wolf whipped around and leapt at something behind us. There was snarling and hissing coming from my left, but I saw nothing through the blackness.

A rancid smell filled the area, and I coughed on it before waving my hand in front of my face. "Someone smells like rotten eggs and needs a bath."

Everything in me screamed "duck."

I listened just as something swiped past my head. I came up fast, as if something else was controlling my actions. The same thing had happened the night of the succu-bitch attack. It had saved my life then, so I wasn't about to look the gift horse in the mouth.

I just went with it, going with whatever felt right.

Spinning, I threw out an elbow and struck something solid. It snarled, and I lifted my other arm fast, blocking a blow from it. Unfortunately, I dropped my phone in the process.

Something grabbed me from behind with such a force that it knocked the wind out of me. It yanked me backward so fast, it was as if I were hooked to a pulley system. My sneakers dragged through the leaves beneath my feet as I struggled for traction.

The snarls and growls grew louder and louder. They were accompanied by a flapping noise that sounded like a hundred birds flying directly at me. I'd never thought to ask Tuck about shadow monsters and bird gangs when grilling him on the supernatural.

If I lived, I'd have to remember to add it to my list.

"You dare to come at her?"

I couldn't place the deep male voice with hints of an accent, but it was familiar. I knew I'd heard it before. I just didn't know when or where. For some reason, the sound of the man's voice was reassuring —like backup had arrived.

I didn't have much time to think more on it all as I found myself being yanked backward in the darkness even faster than before. Images of being taken to some den of darkness to be the thing's lunch filled my head.

"I'm not going out like that, buttmunch," I said through gritted teeth.

Instincts continued to lead, and I lifted my legs, causing the distribution of my weight to change. Whatever had ahold of me let go long enough for me to turn fast and throw a punch. I struck flesh, and it felt a lot like a jaw to me. A slimy one but a jaw all the same.

Something sharp raked over my upper arm, where my armband was, tearing it away and, from the hot, burning sensation in my arm, tearing my flesh as well. A hiss came from me, but I didn't back down. There was no way in hell I was going out by way of a shadow monster.

"Dana!" yelled the man, clearly knowing me. "You're bleeding. How hurt are you?"

How in the world had the maybe-stranger known I was bleeding? I couldn't see a thing. How could he?

"Run!" he yelled.

The thing in front of me swiped out again, catching the same arm but lower.

Now I was good and pissed. I went hard at whatever the hell was attacking me. It managed to get in a nice hit on the side of my face, which caused my head to snap back, but I didn't let that deter me. I punched it twice in rapid succession, knocking it back enough to deliver a wicked kick. It went down, and I grabbed out in the darkness, and came in direct contact with its head.

With one fast snap, I ended the attack, backing up fast, my adrenaline still high.

"Elis, handle the ones in the back!" the man yelled. "Brian, take the other side!"

"I can't see anything," said another man.

"Me either," added yet another.

"Where are they all coming from?" asked a third man. This time, I knew the voice's owner. I'd met him two nights back.

Austin Van Helsing.

"The caves," said the man with the slight accent. "Austin, protect Dana."

"Okay, but where is she?" asked Austin.

"Where is my wolf?" demanded Accent Man. "He's injured. Find him. Get him to safety."

Something tackled me from the side, and I hit the ground with a thud that shuddered through me. It hurt, but it also ticked me off. I rammed my elbow into it again and again. When it loosened its hold on me, I flipped it onto its back and began whaling on it. The smell of it nearly drove me to stop and get away, but I wasn't about to quit until I knew it wasn't a threat anymore.

"I can't find her," said Austin, a second before I heard a grunt then something hit the leaves hard.

"Austin, get up and get to Dana!" shouted the man with the slight accent.

"Uh, trying here. Tripped over a body. Dana, that better not be your body. He'll rip my head off if it is."

I hit the thing under me again for good measure.

"It's not her," said Accent Man, his voice sounding calm all of a sudden, even though it was evident he was fighting with something. Maybe more than one something. "Walk forward twelve paces. She's there—and currently beating a ghoul to a bloody pulp."

"Ghoul?" I echoed as the thing under me quit moving. "You people have got to be joking. Ghouls are real too? Hold up—what exactly is a ghoul, and why does it smell so bad? Ohmygod, am I straddling a zombie?" I scurried off the thing under me and landed unceremoniously on my hip on the ground. I then went to work trying to wipe zombie off me, all while not totally freaking out.

Easier said than done.

"They're not zombies—*exactly*." Austin snickered, and it was cut short as he yelped. "Ouch! I walked into a tree."

There was a heavy sigh, followed by the man

with a slight accent speaking once more. "Austin, step to your left. Then continue forward. She is there, on the ground. Get to her and take her to safety."

"How can you see in this?" questioned Austin.

I wondered the same thing. I also wanted to know what the heck a ghoul actually was.

"You did not seriously ask *him* that," said one of the other men. "I mean, really?"

"Never mind. Stupid question," said Austin. "Dana?"

"Present," I returned, pushing to my feet, fairly confident the thing I'd been whaling on wasn't getting up again anytime soon. I was going to need to shower for a week after this just to get the not-quite-a-zombie off me. "Austin?"

"Here," he said.

That meant nothing to me since I couldn't see him.

"I found Harker!" shouted another. "He's in bad shape!"

There was a commotion not far from me and for a moment, all I heard was a mixture of growls, snarls, and hissing. Then the sound of birds returned a second before someone picked me up and moved me behind them. That was saying something, considering I was hardly petite. But whoever had lifted me didn't seem the least bit fazed by the fact I enjoyed more than salad in my life and towered over most people. In truth, I got the impression I was short compared to him.

There was a whacking noise that sounded wet, and I was a hundred percent positive I did not want to see what caused it.

"You should not have come here," the man with the slight accent said.

I sighed. "Yes, I get it now. Running in the woods in a town full of supernaturals wasn't my smartest move. Neither was running after the black wolf. Can we lecture me later, and can someone explain what, exactly, a ghoul is? And who is Kel? How hurt is he?"

"He was not speaking to you, *woman*," said a new voice. It had a creep factor of ten and was decidedly male. It was heavily accented and reminded me of a campy B-movie villain overdoing a Dracula voice.

"'Move to Grimm Cove,' they said. 'It will be a great change of pace,' they said," I pushed out in a sarcastic tone. It was a coping mechanism.

"Your issue is with me, not her," said the man with the slight accent, still standing in front of me from the sound of his voice. "She is not part of this world."

"She is here. *She* answered the summons you sent out months ago, for those you commanded to return to the fold," said B-Movie Guy. "Therefore, she is very much part of this world."

"She did not answer a summons," said the man in front of me. "It's merely a coincidence that her arrival timed with the summons."

The creepy dude laughed, and it took his villain rating right to eleven. "You are old. You know as well as I that there is no such thing as coincidence. Your summons called to her. She no doubt felt compelled to come here—to Grimm Cove. To you."

"Ha," I said without really thinking about it. "I don't even know him. Well, I don't *think* I know him. And I resent the notion that I gave up a great career and my life in New York to run to a man. That is so beneath me."

The man in front of me chuckled slightly.

"She has your defiant streak, Abraham," said the creepy dude. "She managed to kill two of my minions, yet my spies tell me she has never been trained as a slayer."

I tensed. Slayer? "Um, not to spoil the whole

evil-villain vibe you have going here, but what are you talking about? And why is it so dark? And what, exactly, is a ghoul? Better yet, if it scratches you, do you become one? Why do they smell so bad?"

"Speak only when spoken to, woman," said the creepy dude.

I told him exactly what I thought of his statement and where he could stick it in the process.

The next I knew, a bunch of guys were laughing—hard. The man in front of me wasn't one of them.

"You must be so proud, Abraham," said creepy dude.

"Actually, I *am* extraordinarily proud of her," said the man with a slight accent. "She is a strong young woman who has accomplished much in her short life."

Short life? I was forty. Not sure how old *he* was.

"I warned you the time would come when you would rue the day you interfered in a feud not your own," said creepy dude.

I snorted, finding the statement way funnier than I should. I understood it was more than likely from shock and stress, but it was amusing all the same.

"Backup comes as we speak," said Abraham. "My wolves tell me other shifters are nearly upon us, Dragos. Call off your demons and let us settle this as men."

"Never," said creepy dude.

Something hit me from behind, and I slammed into the man in front of me. It was a lot like running face first into a brick wall. It hurt. A lot.

He twisted around just as whatever had hit me jerked me back. I lost my footing, and so did whatever had me. We went down hard and I rolled.

It followed and ended up on top of me. I went to strike, only to hear growling off to my right. It grew louder—and suddenly the weight of whatever had been on me was gone.

I pushed to my feet quickly and listened to my gut when it told me to move from the spot I was in. I did and felt something brush by me.

Snarls rent the air, and whatever was happening near me sounded vicious. I was kind of glad I couldn't see it all. Then again, my imagination wasn't coming up with a scenario that wasn't horrifying, so it wasn't a ton of help either.

My hand acted of its own accord, going up just in time to catch what felt like a fist in midair. I had half a second to think about how cool the move had been before I was kneeing someone in the groin. Whoever had been there was ripped away.

There was more snarling and growling.

"Jeffrey! Dana!" yelled Brett, sounding close. "Stratton, do you see them?"

"I can't see anything!" yelled another man.

No sooner had the words left his mouth than the darkness began to recede. It was as if someone had a giant vacuum and was sucking it outward, away from us.

When it was gone, I was left standing there with dead creatures littering the forest floor.

Brett wasn't more than twenty feet from me, his eyes wide as he looked at the scene. "Are those…?"

An attractive man who was dressed a lot like the men I worked with back in New York stood near him. He nodded. "Ghouls."

"Shit," said Brett in a hushed breath.

The other man inclined his head in a way that said he shared Brett's sentiment. "Have you had issues with them in Grimm Cove before?"

I noticed Austin and the other men I'd heard talking in the darkness were nowhere to be seen. Neither was the creepy dude. And neither was the black wolf. All that was left behind were ghoul bodies and me.

"Not in my lifetime," said Brett before looking up at me. "Dana! You're hurt!"

I glanced at my upper arm to find it was indeed bleeding. I wasn't worried about it. I was worried about Jeffrey, though. Brett had called his name only moments before, but I didn't see him anywhere. "Is he hurt?"

Confused, Brett tipped his head. "Who?"

"Jeffrey," I said, jumping over one of the dead creatures on the ground, fearing I'd find Jeffrey among them. There was a pile of more than one ghoul, and my heart leapt to my throat as I rushed to it. I bent fast and pushed one off the top. He wasn't there, and I let out a breath I'd not realized I'd been holding.

"Dana, stop, he's fine," said Brett. "I swear to you he's not among the dead."

My brain felt as though it were on autopilot as I twisted around, despite Brett's words of assurance, and checked other bodies on the ground for any sign of Jeffrey.

While I didn't find him, I did find a huge honey-colored wolf running right at me.

I rose quickly and froze.

Brett was suddenly in front of me. "Farkas, no!

Get ahold of your wolf. She's alive. Banged up but alive."

I leaned around him to see the honey-colored wolf narrowing its gaze on Brett. It snarled.

Brett tensed. "Don't do this. I don't want to fight with you, but I will to keep her safe. You don't want her hurt. Your emotions are high. Take a beat here. Stratton?"

"Yes, Chief?" asked the attractive man.

"Take Dana back to the house," said Brett. "I need to get Jeffrey under control."

I continued to stare at the honey-colored wolf. It had icy blue eyes. The same color as Jeffrey's when he'd lost control on the porch before my run had started. As I put together the wolf was Jeffrey, I gasped. "Holy crap. You so *can* totally lick your own butt!"

The wolf's expression went from dark and dangerous to relaxed. He then crouched partially, and I grabbed Brett's arm as I watched the wolf change from animal to man.

A very naked man.

Jeffrey stood fully, cupping himself in the process. Looked to be a handful.

It took me a moment to realize Brett's head was turned and he was staring at me as I stood pressed against his back, clinging to his arm as I peeked around him to gawk at Jeffrey. I lifted a brow. "That was awesome! Can he do it again? Does he know any tricks? Fetch. Is he good at fetch?"

Brett groaned. "You're going to be just fine."

I stepped out from behind him, and Jeffrey gasped.

"You're hurt," he said, making a move to come toward me. In the process, he stopped cupping himself as he reached for me.

My gaze snapped to his groin.

Never had I wanted to play stuff the cannoli more in my life.

He stopped quickly and reached down again, cupping himself once more. "Sorry."

"Nothing to apologize for," I said, my gaze still locked on his groin area.

Brett took me gently by the shoulders and turned me around to face away from Jeffrey.

"Mood killer," I said with a huff.

Brett snorted. "Sorry about that."

"No, you're not," I returned, wanting very much to turn and see the rest of the show. Instead, I continued to face away from Jeffrey, staring at Stratton in his stead.

Stratton was in the process of removing his

dress shirt.

My brows went up. "This slow striptease and Jeffrey's naked display are gifts for enduring Grimm Cove, aren't they? Brett, don't get naked. I won't be able to look you in the eyes when we're home, knowing everything you bring to the table."

He chuckled. "I'll do my best."

"Good. But from the way Poppy sounds through the walls at night, you bring a *lot* to said table," I returned.

He groaned again.

I soaked in my fill of Stratton as he finished removing his outer shirt. His undershirt pulled up slightly, revealing a chiseled torso.

His gaze snapped to me.

I winked.

He grinned.

There was a growl from behind me.

"Stop putting on a show for her," snapped Jeffrey, his voice sounding much deeper than normal.

Stratton went even slower with his actions, purposely lifting his undershirt again. I half expected the man to begin to move his hips to an invisible beat and offer the Full Monty.

It was hard not to laugh. I knew I had an excess

of adrenaline combined with a hefty dose of shock going for me. Nervous laughing and sexual innuendos were apparently the end result.

Good to know I was maturing in my forties.

Jeffrey's growl grew louder.

I heard Brett grunting next. "Stop. You're not allowed to attack my detective."

"Why not?" demanded Jeffrey.

"Give me a minute while I try to think of a good reason," said Brett.

Stratton grinned wider. He held the shirt up in a dramatic fashion and then tossed it in the direction of Jeffrey. "Here. No one wants to walk out of here with you naked."

"Speak for yourself," I said quickly.

"Oh a wild one," he returned. "I like it."

"Put the damn shirt around you, Farkas, and stop trying to go at Stratton," said Brett, adding his own growl to the mix. "I don't want to explain to my wife why I let you run around in the buck with her best friend."

"Poppy won't mind," I said with a shrug, knowing my friend well. "She'll be disappointed she missed it though."

"That's it," snapped Brett. "Put the shirt on, Jeffrey, or I'll tie it around your neck."

"I'm alpha here," warned Jeffrey.

"Fine. Then act like it. Stop getting baited into something by Stratton." Brett sounded tired. "Your head is screwed on backward right now. Get a grip, brother."

I locked gazes with Stratton. "Does your boss ever let you have any fun?"

"Occasionally," he replied with a sexy wink.

Try as I might to pretend there wasn't a bunch of dead ghouls at our feet, I couldn't help but glance down. When I did, my stomach knotted. Something had torn one of the ghouls apart. I swallowed hard, glad I hadn't eaten yet today.

Stratton motioned to the creatures on the ground and then at me. "You killed all of these ghouls? There has to be at least thirty here. Maybe more." He seemed impressed.

Unfortunately, I couldn't take credit for it all.

"No. I only killed a couple of them," I said, becoming acutely aware of how easily that statement had rolled off my tongue. Three days ago, the most I'd killed were spiders and cockroaches (par for the course in the buildings I grew up in). All that had changed upon my arrival in Grimm Cove. I was now racking up a body count that made me wonder if Mafia really was in my blood.

Who knew I'd end up being the most dangerous person to come from the old neighborhood?

"Dana," said Jeffrey from directly behind me, as Brett stepped around me to get closer to the pile of dead ghouls.

I turned to find Jeffrey had tied the shirt around his waist. It looked a bit like a kilt. Now that certain aspects of his very gifted body weren't commanding my attention, I noticed just how ripped the guy was. I could have done laundry off his abs.

Jeffrey eased closer, and my breath caught.

He touched just below my chin, directing my gaze to his. "How hurt are you?"

"A little scratched up. That's all," I said, lessening the distance between us. I was left pressed to him.

His body was hot to the touch, as if he'd just come from a sauna.

"Do you have a fever?" I blurted, worried for him.

"No, Legs," he said in a low tone. "My body runs hotter as a shifter, and I'm worked up."

It took me a second to realize he was shaking slightly. "Jeffrey?"

"I was so worried about you," he said, his voice barely there.

My hands went to his bare chest. "I'm okay."

He inhaled deeply and his eyes shifted to icy blue again.

This time it didn't catch me off guard.

Without overthinking it, I wrapped my arms around his waist and put my cheek to his chest. It wasn't like me to seek comfort from a man. In truth, I saw it as a personal weakness, but I didn't care. In that moment, I needed what he provided— a sense of security.

His arms shot around me and he squeezed me tight, his lips finding my forehead. "Legs, never scare me like that again."

I smiled against his chest and I continued to hold him.

The act wasn't something I was known for.

Surprised even me.

TWELVE

Jeffrey

JEFFREY HELD DANA TO HIM, afraid to let her go. He'd feared he'd arrive too late. That when he found her, she'd be hurt or dead. Then, when he had finally reached her, it was only to find her blanketed in dark magik. The darkness had been so thick and so strong that even his wolf side had issues seeing in it.

But he'd smelled her there, and he'd sensed she'd been injured. Now, seeing he was right, that she had been hurt, he wanted to bring each and every one of the things that hurt her back to life only to kill them himself. He'd tear them limb from limb, much like the ghoul nearest them had been.

As her lips met his bare chest, Jeffrey's body reacted. The shirt tied around his waist did little to hide his arousal. The smell of mint and citrus assailed him, leaving a low rumble coming deep from within his chest. He tightened his hold on Dana. The thin material of her running clothes only served to make him harder.

Now wasn't the time or place for any of that. Too bad his lower region hadn't caught on to that fact.

He tried to will it away.

That didn't work.

Dana put her forehead to his chest and sighed. "It all happened so fast. Everything was fine and then it was pitch black."

"You had to be scared," he said before remembering who he was talking to. She was fierce, and he highly doubted she'd admit to being afraid.

"I was torn between running and making peace with what I was sure was my end," she confessed, surprising him. "Then I remembered that I'd managed to make it through a vampire attack. Shadow monsters were not going to be how I went out."

Her ability to find dark humor during a trying time made him smile. The next he knew, he was kissing the top of her head and then closing his eyes, continuing to hold her tightly to him.

He felt the weight of someone's stare on him and opened his eyes to find his best friend looking dumbfounded. Brett was standing there, his mouth agape as he blinked at Jeffrey.

Stratton strolled up alongside Brett. "You look thunderstruck."

"I am," said Brett. "Never seen him behave this way over a woman before."

With a shrug, Stratton bent near a dead body. "He's not acting out of line for a shifter whose mate was in danger. I'm more shocked that he hasn't tried to club her over the head and drag her off to a wolf den while shouting 'mine.'"

Jeffrey stiffened, jerking Dana against him harder.

She grunted.

His mate?

No.

That couldn't be.

Could it?

He thought about the overwhelming urge he'd had to get to her. How his sole driving force was protecting her. Then he thought about what it had felt like when he'd first met her—when she'd punched him in the face. And how he'd spent two days basically begging her to go out with him.

His eyes widened, but he didn't release her even as the realization that Stratton's words weren't misguided struck him. They were right. The woman before him was his mate. It was the only thing that made sense.

Brett blinked several times. "Is she…?"

"Am I what?" asked Dana, easing back from Jeffrey somewhat. She glanced at his arm. "I got blood on you. Sorry."

He'd have focused more on the mate thing, but worry for her took root in him once more. He reached for her injured arm to assess the damage. What he found confused him. "You were hurt a minute ago. I know because I saw it with my own eyes."

She nodded. "Yes. The not-exactly-a-zombie ghoul thing slashed my arm open."

He ran his thumb over her upper arm. There was nothing there any longer. No torn flesh. No sign, other than blood, that she'd ever been injured. "Look."

She did. She then whipped around to face Brett. "Ohmygod, am I a ghoul now? Am I going to smell like that? Will I look like that?" Dana nudged the body of the ghoul closest to her with her foot, her nose wrinkling as she did. She also stared harder at the ghoul. "Is it me, or is it kind of greenish? Ohmygod, I'm going to turn into the Wicked Witch of the West!"

Brett appeared confused as he shook his head. "What? No. You're not a ghoul. Why would you think that?"

"Because I've seen movies. Get bit by a vampire, you're a vampire. Get bit by a werewolf and the next full moon, you can lick your own butt. I got scratched by a ghoul. I think one drooled on me too. Therefore, I'm a ghoul now."

Jeffrey nearly laughed at the way her mind worked, but he reminded himself that she hadn't grown up in Grimm Cove, where supernaturals were the norm. "Legs, it doesn't work that way."

She pointed to her arm. "How did that heal so fast then?"

"I don't know," he said. "But I'm happy it did."

Brett cleared his throat. "Dana, did you heal that quickly after the vampire attack?"

"I didn't get hurt in the vampire attack," she said.

Stratton was still bent near one of the creatures. "How fast do you normally heal?"

Dana was quiet a moment before she tensed. "I, um, have never been hurt before today that I can remember. I mean, I've stubbed my toe and done things like that, but nothing that would require stitches or something."

Stratton stood. His gaze set on her. "What are you? I sense magik in you. It's faint but there. It's not your strong suit. What is?"

She scoffed. "I'm human. Unless you believe Marcy, who claims my grandmother is a witch. Which is totally and completely absurd."

"Is it?" asked Stratton. He motioned to the bodies littering the ground. "How do you explain this? Humans can't kill a ghoul with any kind of ease, on a clear day, with perfect conditions. When we got on the scene, there was dark magik coating the area. It was pitch black. We couldn't see anything. Could you?"

"No," she said. She then stepped closer to Jeffrey once more.

He put his hand on her shoulder. "What is it, Legs?"

"But I kind of sensed things. I just felt something coming at my face, put a hand outward, and caught a fist before it hit me," she confessed. "That was odd. Are we sure I wasn't infected with ghoulishness?"

"We're sure," said the men together.

Jeffrey rubbed her shoulder. "Legs, I'm not so sure your grandmother's claim of being a witch is absurd. Do you know anything about your grandfather? Or your father?"

She was quiet a moment. "Nonna doesn't talk a lot about my grandfather. I never knew him. All I know is, he apparently liked to hunt a lot. She's mentioned hunting a number of times over the years. That's about it for him."

Jeffrey's gaze snapped to Brett's.

Brett shook his head faintly. "You don't think her grandfather was a hunter, do you?"

"I already said he liked to hunt," added Dana, sounding exasperated.

Jeffrey drew her closer to him. "Legs, he means hunter as in slayer. The terms are often interchangeable. A slayer is someone who is born with the ability to stand against the supernatural. To go toe to toe with us. To police us, if you will."

"Dragos said something about slayers," she said, her voice low.

"Who?" asked Jeffrey.

"Some creepy dude with a campy voice. He was here, telling that Abraham guy he'd rue the day he interfered in a feud that wasn't his own. He even accused the guy of summoning me to Grimm Cove months ago," she said with a shrug.

"Others were here?" asked Jeffrey, looking at Brett. "Did you sense them?"

"I couldn't sense or smell much when we got here," admitted Brett. "The stench from the ghouls was overpowering. But I didn't hear anyone else either."

Stratton examined another body. "There was at least one vampire here. *I* can sense it. Maybe more. The other kill back that way was from a shifter, but I don't think it was you, Jeffrey. I think another wolf-shifter was here. I noticed paw prints that way too, but they don't match yours."

Dana lifted a hand. "The black wolf? Where is it? I hope he wasn't hurt. I ran after him but lost sight of him when the darkness came. Then everything happened so fast that I forgot about him. I'd like it noted I'd make a horrible pet owner. I can't keep anything safe and alive. I need to find him."

She went to move away from Jeffrey, but he caught her, keeping her close. "Legs, there are no other wolves here except for Brett and me."

She faced him fully. "There *was* a big black wolf here. It was here before the darkness came. I think it was trying to protect me—maybe even warn me away from the area."

"None of our pack was near here recently. I'd know," said Jeffrey, and he would. As alpha, he was very aware of his pack members and could sense them with ease. "Anyone know a Dragos or an Abraham?"

"No," said Brett.

Stratton checked another body. "I've heard stories about them. So have you. I thought they were myths."

Jeffrey shook his head. "I don't know of any myths about them."

Stratton retrieved something from the ground near the closest body. "Sure you do. Stoker wrote about it. Well, kind of."

Jeffrey's mind raced, and he snorted. "Bram Stoker? Dracula? Are you telling me Stoker's story about Dracula was real and that the famed vampire is here in Grimm Cove? I can turn into a wolf, and I have trouble believing there is a real, honest-to-God Dracula."

"Not exactly," said Stratton.

Dana huffed. "You people like to give that explanation a lot."

"Us people?" he asked.

She nodded. "Grimm Cove people. That is the second time I've heard it this morning."

Stratton didn't seem fazed. "About Stoker, he didn't tell the entire story. And he dressed it all up as fiction. In reality, there was a chunk of it that was true to some extent. Other parts were wrong. From the way I heard it said, this was done on purpose. For instance, the part about how Dracula, or Vlad, came to be a vampire. From what I was told, it wasn't from turning against God. It was because he and his young wife were attacked by a demon. A demon that lived off blood. One with the power to call forth other demons to serve him. Mindless hordes whose stench could be smelled for days later. Dracula survived—if you can call it that —ending up a vampire. His young wife did not live."

"Are you saying the demon who made Dracula is here?" asked Jeffrey, wanting to be sure he was following the man's wild logic. "That it and its smelly horde are in Grimm Cove, and that they attacked Dana?"

"I'm saying it's a distinct possibility. Dragos's name has come up more than once in various stories of the supernatural I've heard over the years. If they're to be believed, he is powerful, feeds off blood, has minions he controls, and possesses dark magik."

That caught Jeffrey's attention. "Enough to blanket this area in darkness?"

"Yes," said Stratton.

"Shit," whispered Brett. "I'm almost afraid to ask who Abraham is then?"

"You could ask Austin," said Dana matter-of-factly. "He knows him."

"What do you mean?" questioned Jeffrey, wanting to know what the manager of his bar had to do with it all.

"Austin was here too. So were some other men," she said, touching her chin. "Let me think. Um, Elis, Harker, and Brian? I think those were the names Abraham said."

A smug smile appeared on Stratton's face. "Believe me now? Or do you think it's coincidence that three Van Helsings just happened to be here as well? And if you read Stoker's story, you'd recognize another surname too. Harker. In the story, Professor Van Helsing's first name was—"

Dana sucked in a big breath. "Abraham."

"You're familiar with the story then?" asked Stratton.

She nodded. "I got teased enough about it

growing up because of my last name. It was really bad when I started dating a guy with the last name Harker in high school."

Jeffrey looked to Brett for clarification. While he'd been hot to trot for the woman, Jeffrey had not actually bothered to ask her surname. Didn't seem imperative.

Now it did.

"Wait. There were three Van Helsings here?" she asked. "Who was the other one?"

"You mean other *two*," corrected Jeffrey.

She shook her head. "No. Austin is one. I'm the other. So, who was the third?"

Jeffrey took a giant step back from her. "What do you mean by *you're* the other?"

She pointed to herself. "Me. Dana Van Helsing."

"*She's* a Van Helsing?" demanded Jeffrey of Brett.

Brett came at him fast. "Calm down. I didn't know. Poppy never mentioned her last name to me, and I didn't think to ask."

"Guys?" asked Dana. "Why is this such a sore issue?"

"Because I hate the Van Helsings," snapped Jeffrey. "*Every* last one of them."

Her posture went rigid, and her green gaze hardened on him. "Is that so?"

Jeffrey opened his mouth to speak, but Brett stepped between him and Dana. He stared at Jeffrey. "Brother, think hard before you open your mouth here. She strike you as the forgiving type?"

"If by 'forgiving' you mean 'has an air about her that says she could rip vital pieces off him,' then *yes*," said Stratton. "Want proof of what she's capable of? She killed two of these ghouls. The rest have indications of large males being responsible or vampires and wolf-shifters. But two have markings on them that said someone with smaller hands than the others did it."

"I'd say I feel bad about doing it, but that would be a lie," said Dana. "Now, Brett, kindly step aside. I very much want to hear all about how much Jeffrey hates *every* last Van Helsing."

With a sigh, Brett moved to the side.

Jeffrey was all set to let her know just how much he loathed the Van Helsings—when he remembered how desperate he'd been to get to her. How worried he'd been that he'd be too late. And how it had felt seeing her arm ripped open.

If he had any doubts as to who she was to him, they vanished. The truth settled over him, and for a split second, it felt like an albatross around the neck.

"You have got to be kidding me!" he shouted. "My mate is a Van Helsing?"

Dana recoiled. "Mate? Like what Brett and Poppy are to each other? Uh, no. I'm not your mate."

"That doesn't seem to be the case," said Jeffrey, the words coming out snider than he'd intended.

THIRTEEN

Jeffrey

"DANA IS JEFFREY'S MATE?" asked Poppy, drawing a round of surprised gasps from every party present.

Jeffrey hadn't heard anyone approaching. That said something in itself. He'd been so fixated on Dana that he'd let his guard down.

Brett's eyes widened. "Poppy-seed, what are you doing out here?"

Poppy and Marcy were just outside of the area where the darkness had been, staring in at the carnage. Poppy appeared stunned and sick to her stomach. She gulped as she stared at the bodies of the ghouls on the ground, and then stepped over one in a way that looked as though she was worried it might come back to life and grab her.

Marcy pinched her nose, stepping over the ghoul as well, staying close to Poppy, their arms looped around one another. "They aren't the best-smelling things, are they?"

Brett leaped over two ghoul bodies at once and raced to his mate. He tried to usher her away from the area, but Poppy wasn't having any of it.

She artfully maneuvered out of her husband's hold and went right for Dana. "You're bleeding!"

Dana tensed. "Um, not really anymore."

Poppy got to Dana and grabbed her, hugging her tight. "I was so worried about you. What happened? You're hurt?"

Dana had to practically pry Poppy from her just to answer. "I got a little turned around on my run, came across a black wolf, freaked out a bit but realized it was a shifter, and I thought he was one of Brett's pack mates."

"He wasn't," said Jeffrey and Brett at the same time.

Dana shot them both dirty looks.

Brett put his hands up. "Sorry. Continue. When you're done, I'm going to give her a piece of my mind about coming out here when she knew damn well there was something dangerous out here."

Marcy went to Brett and pushed lightly on him, pointing to one of the dead ghouls. "What is it?"

"Ghoul," said Brett.

"Do they always smell like a mix of sulfur and rotten eggs?" she asked. "I once knew a man who lived two apartments down from mine when I was calling San Francisco home. He smelled the same. He didn't really converse so much as he moaned and grunted. Think he was a ghoul?" she questioned, clearly keeping Brett occupied with questions while Poppy spoke with Dana.

It worked.

Marcy perked, seeming excited. "A worm just crawled out of that one's eye."

Just then, the same bluebird she'd named on the porch of the Proctor House, the one that had whistled and walked back and forth, came swooping down. It grabbed the worm and took flight again.

Marcy smiled. "The ghoul is giving back to nature. That was sweet of him. Rogelio deserved a treat for letting us know Dana was in danger. It was really nice of the ghoul to give him one. When I was younger, I'd keep worms in my pocket for birds but once I forgot about them and they went through the wash. That didn't turn out well."

Brett glanced at Jeffrey and quirked a brow.

Jeffrey shook his head. There was no figuring the woman out. She clearly lived in her own version of reality.

"Where are you hurt?" demanded Poppy of Dana.

"I'm not hurt anymore," returned Dana cautiously.

Poppy tipped her head. "I don't understand. That isn't your blood all over your arm?"

"No. It's my blood," said Dana, swallowing hard. "I just, well, I was hurt but now I'm not. One of those smelly not-exactly-a-zombie things ripped the heck out of my upper arm, more than once. But then it just sort of healed over instantly, pretty much."

Poppy grabbed Dana's hands while she looked to Brett. "Ohmygod, is Dana infected with ghoul?"

Stratton laughed and tried to hide it with a cough. "Don't mind me. Easy to see why they're friends. They think alike."

"Is she?" asked Poppy, her voice rising two octaves.

"She's not," said Jeffrey before Brett could get the chance. He was still being tugged and pushed away from Poppy by Marcy.

Jeffrey had to hand it to Marcy, she was handy at diverting the man's attention.

Poppy stared at him. "Why do you look mad about the fact she's not infected with stinky ghoul?"

"He apparently hates all Van Helsings," answered Dana, the fight leaving her voice. "Me included, since I'm one."

For some reason, that bothered Jeffrey more than it should. He didn't like knowing she didn't care enough to snap back at him. If that fire in her wasn't burning, did that mean she was indifferent to him?

"I don't understand. If you're her mate, how can you hate her? And can I just point out how much you didn't seem to hate her when you were at the house, doing your best to pry information out of me about her?" Poppy questioned, sounding as if she'd caught all of Dana's inner fire and was now directing it at Jeffrey. "And why are you wearing nothing but a…is that a skirt?"

"It's a shirt." He exhaled slowly. "And the rest is complicated."

Poppy stared harder at him. "Seems simple to me. Is she your mate or not, Jeffrey?"

"Not," said Dana, her voice barely there.

"She's my mate," said Jeffrey evenly.

"I'd argue with you, but I'm exhausted. I need to wash ghoul off me, and then I need to figure out who Abraham is, because his voice was kind of familiar to me. I can't place it, though. Plus, he acted like he knew me. Said he was proud of me, even. And he was really worried about me getting to safety and Dragos staying away from me," said Dana, making a move to walk away.

Poppy kept hold of her hands. "And you don't know who Abraham is?"

"No," she said. "But he was here, along with Austin and some other guys."

Poppy gasped. "Austin attacked you? He seemed so nice. Did you take him? I bet you could take him."

"No. The ghouls and some guy named Dragos attacked me. Abraham, Austin, and the others showed up to help protect me."

"And you think Abraham's voice is familiar?" asked Poppy. "Did you recognize his face too?"

"Never saw it," replied Dana, sounding tired. "The whole area was pitch black. Couldn't see my hand in front of my face even."

Jeffrey stepped in her direction, wanting to go to her. The need to offer her comfort was nearly all-consuming. "Dana."

She didn't look at him.

Poppy continued to hold her hands. "I'm so sorry that I brought you here. I didn't know it would be this way."

"It's not your fault," assured Dana. "I wanted to come to Grimm Cove. I felt this weird pull to come here, which I'm starting to think wasn't by accident. Can we head back to the house now? I want to wash ghoul off me."

Poppy released Dana's hands and reached up, pulling a bit of something from Dana's ponytail. Poppy wrinkled her nose and tossed it aside. "Yuck."

Dana's gaze followed. "Did I have ghoul in my hair?"

"I think so," said Poppy.

Dana groaned. "Of course I did. Why not?"

"Come on, we'll get you cleaned up and make sure you're not hurt but maybe don't know it because of shock," said Poppy. "And if it helps, I'll look through my grandmother's spell books that Marcy's been reading to see if there is a spell to keep Jeffrey away from you."

"Poppy," he said quickly. "You'd do that? I thought we were friends."

She leveled her gaze on him. "She's like a sister

to me. I'd do *anything* for her. You'd do well to remember that."

He nodded.

Dana touched Poppy's arm. "Don't do any weird witchy stuff to him. I'm fine with him hating me because of my surname. It doesn't matter what he thinks of me. I haven't decided if I'm going to stay in Grimm Cove or not. Because I'm not sure if you guys realize just how insane this town really is. You should really have people sign waivers at the city limits or something. Check here if you understand there is a one hundred percent chance you will be attacked by some kind of demon."

"You want to leave?" asked Jeffrey, the fight leaking out of him. He wasn't exactly pleased to find out she was a Van Helsing, but he didn't want her gone. He just wanted a minute to wrap his mind around the idea that he had a mate, and she just so happened to share a last name with the douchebag known as Elis.

"Can you blame her, Jeffrey?" snapped Poppy with so much bite, Jeffrey thought she might challenge him to head the pack. She was that fierce. In her current state, she just might win.

He sighed. "No. I can't blame her."

"Do you want her to stay?" demanded Poppy.

"Maybe Dana and I should discuss this later," said Jeffrey, wanting to get away from the audience they currently had.

Poppy glanced around at the dead ghouls and then right back at him. "They're not going anywhere anytime soon, by the looks of it. Now is the perfect time. Speak your truth, Jeffrey. I'll speak mine. I love her. She's family to me. I want her to stay but I'll respect her wishes if she wants to leave. And right now, I'm trying very hard not to pick up a ghoul body part and beat you with it for being a thick-headed moron."

"Poppy-seed?" asked Brett, finally managing to get free of Marcy's questions. "Did you just threaten Jeffrey with dead ghoul parts?"

"You should use the arm of one," said Marcy, walking toward Stratton. "It's lighter than a leg and will be more effective at injuring Jeffrey than a ghoul head or something."

"Thanks for all the support, Marcy," said Jeffrey.

Marcy met his gaze. "She's like a sister to me too."

Stratton chuckled. "In other words, mess with one and you get all three gunning for you."

"Yes," said Marcy and Poppy.

Dana remained quiet.

Marcy tipped her head. "We're her backup bitches. And we're not above bludgeoning you to death with ghoul parts. Plus, I know a gal who knows a gal—in other words, I have mob connections."

"You cannot ask my grandmother to hide his body," said Dana.

"Why not? She would," said Marcy.

Poppy did a double take in her friend's direction and then reached for Dana once more. "Come on, hon."

Dana took three steps, and Jeffrey found himself moving forward after her. "Do you want to leave Grimm Cove?"

What he really wanted to ask was if she wanted to leave *him*, but the words wouldn't form.

"I don't know what I want," she said firmly, refusing to face him. "Do you know what you want? Because you're hot and cold with me."

All eyes went to him.

"I, um, well…like I said. It's complicated," he managed, suddenly afraid of three women.

Dana rounded on him fully, a hand going to her hip.

Damn, the woman made being angry sexy.

Why did she have to be a Van Helsing?

"Well?" she demanded. "Are you going to deny running hot and cold with me?"

He fidgeted with the shirt sleeves, making sure they were tied tight, wanting to avoid answering in front of everyone. He didn't like looking weak. "I don't know what you mean."

"I call bull," said Marcy from her spot near Stratton. She glanced at the tree near her. "Oh, a caterpillar."

Stratton simply shook his head.

Jeffrey found he was unable to escape Dana's penetrating gaze. As she jutted out her chin in defiance, he knew he'd more than overstepped his bounds with her. He'd catapulted over them.

She huffed. "I'm going to go ahead and assume our breakfast date is off. As are any other possible ones."

He opened his mouth to protest but she didn't let him get a word in edgewise.

"You know where you can stick your hatred of all Van Helsings?" she asked.

Poppy grabbed for her and reached up fast, putting her hand over Dana's mouth. She then gave Jeffrey a knowing look.

"What a shame," said Marcy. "She'd have given

you a chance before. But, like we said, when she tells you where to stick things, it's a hard no from her."

Jeffrey's wolf stirred deep in him, making him aware it wasn't happy with him either.

Everyone's a critic.

"I've been here forty-eight hours, and in that time, I've been attacked twice by things that shouldn't even be real. I've been drooled on by a not-exactly-a-zombie. I've been sliced open by one. And the town is apparently running over with Van Helsings. Never met another one in all forty years I've been alive, and then I find two others here," offered Dana.

"More than two," said Stratton as Marcy stepped closer to him. "There are a good number of them. Elis, Brian, and Austin are all Van Helsings. And if I'm right, so is Abraham."

"Then why haven't we met him before?" asked Brett, making his way to his wife. He put an arm around her protectively. "The Van Helsings are pretty tight. And I'd like to point out the obvious, that Stoker's book is how old? Slayers don't live that long. So this Abraham guy can't be the same one Stoker wrote about."

"Stoker's book?" asked Poppy, confusion

coating her expression.

Marcy edged so close to Stratton that they were now pressed together.

Stratton looked afraid to move for fear he might set off the crazy lady.

"Abraham Van Helsing is the professor from Bram Stoker's book, *Dracula*," said Marcy, sounding totally sane. "We should have a Dracula theme party and invite all of our vampire neighbors. It's important to make them feel welcome too. Burgess would love it. I could make him a tiny cape to wear. He'd be adorable in it."

And just like that, the sanity left.

"So you think the Abraham who came to help Dana is the one Stoker wrote about?" asked Poppy.

"Possibly," said Stratton.

"I agree with Brett. He'd be dead by now." Poppy stepped closer to her mate.

"True, but that's assuming he's a slayer or human and not something else," said Stratton. "Lots of questions."

"And no real answers," said Brett before motioning toward one of the dead ghouls. "We need to get teams out here to make this all go away. Stratton, can you reach out to the usual suspects, get that started?"

He nodded. "Can do, boss. Question though."

"What's that?" asked Brett.

"You guys never found it curious that you have a bunch of Van Helsings here, with the same name as a supposedly fictitious vampire slayer, and that these Van Helsings just so happen to run around town with a guy whose surname is Harker?"

Jeffrey and Brett shared a look. Clearly neither had given that much thought, in the past.

"Harker?" asked Marcy. "Is his name Jonathan, like in the book?"

"No," said Brett. "Different Harker."

She shrugged and returned to focusing on the caterpillar.

Brett looked to Dana. "Something isn't sitting right with me. You mentioned your father passed away when you were little."

Poppy elbowed her mate. "Brett."

Dana nodded. "He did. I was just a baby still. No one in my family really talks about it. I don't know anything about him or his side of the family. I've asked over the years, but my mom and my grandmother were tight-lipped about him."

"What was his name?" asked Jeffrey.

"Bram Van Helsing," she said.

FOURTEEN

Jeffrey

JEFFREY'S entire body tensed as he thought harder about Dana's father's name. As much as he didn't want to believe it was true, the pieces fit. "Bram, as in the short form of Abraham?"

"Yes," said Marcy, bending to touch the dead ghoul nearest her and Stratton.

Stratton bent alongside Marcy and moved her hand before she could make contact with the dead ghoul.

Poppy's eyes widened. "You think he's...?"

Brett sucked in a big breath. "It's a big leap but my gut is saying we're on the right track."

"On the right track with what?" asked Dana. She didn't say another word for a moment as everyone simply stared at her.

Poppy offered a sympathetic smile. "I'm sure they're wrong. Your grandmother and mother wouldn't have lied to you about something like that."

"What do you…?" Dana stiffened. "You think Abraham is my father?"

Brett and Jeffrey nodded hesitantly.

Dana snorted loudly. "Yeah, right. That would mean my father has been alive all this time, and my mother and my grandmother spent my life lying to me? Next, you'll tell me my father was the black wolf. Or maybe a ghoul who smelled better. Or hey, how about a vampire? Because you're suggesting he's freaking immortal."

All the men shared a look at the mention of him being a vampire. It would fit. Vampires had immortality on their side. It stood to reason he could very well have been alive in Stoker's time. And he'd be considered the living dead. Not to mention, if Stoker's book was born from a grain of truth, could it be that Abraham Van Helsing was turned into a vampire too?

Poppy pointed to Jeffrey, and then Brett. "I know you two. You're both thinking the same thing. What is it?"

"Maybe they didn't lie to Dana," said Jeffrey. "Maybe they bent the truth trying to protect her."

Marcy nodded, making yet another move to touch the ghoul.

Stratton sighed and took her hand in his, holding it as he stood fully, taking her with him. He kept hold of her hand as if she were a child.

Dana's brows met. "Bent the truth? Elaborate."

"Dana, some don't consider vampires to be alive in the normal sense of the word," Jeffrey said, wanting to hold her despite her being a Van Helsing.

In fact, the more he thought about her leaving Grimm Cove for good, the less he cared what her last name was.

"I'd like to go home now," she said to Poppy, ignoring Jeffrey as she turned and walked away.

He hurried to her, coming to a stop right behind her. "Legs."

She paused but didn't face him.

"Want me to break his kneecaps?" asked Brett with a slight laugh.

Dana chuckled weakly. "Maybe."

"Legs, look at me. Please," Jeffrey pleaded.

She glanced over her shoulder at him, her green

gaze seeing right through to his soul. Her eyes were rimmed with red and moist. He knew tears were close to falling, and that everything she'd had thrown at her since arriving in town had been too much for her.

If he dared to let her walk away, she'd walk clean out of his life for good.

He knew it in his bones.

That wasn't an option.

The woman had blown into his life like a tornado, turning his world upside down, and he didn't want to go back to the way it had been before her—the other women, the reckless behavior. He wanted to grab her with both hands and not let go.

Right now, if he tried that, she'd no doubt remove vital bits.

"Sometimes, when I speak, it's without thinking," he said.

"*Sometimes*?" she asked. "Just sometimes?"

"Most of the time," he corrected, earning him the slightest of smiles from her. He licked his lips. "I don't want you to leave Grimm Cove."

"Why?" she asked, narrowing her gaze on him.

"Because you're his mate," said Marcy, answering for him.

He lifted a hand in her direction. "What she said."

"That's the *only* reason?" asked Dana. "Because you have some misguided notion that I'm your special someone? I'm not."

"You don't feel any pull to him?" asked Poppy, sounding disappointed.

Dana glanced at her. "I just feel the urge to go for his kneecaps. Does that count?"

Brett snorted.

Jeffrey groaned.

His best friend shrugged. "What? We already discussed the fact she'd rip vital pieces off. Be happy she only wants to go at your kneecaps. As you pointed out, you're not really wearing anything to help protect *other* parts."

Well, there was that.

Jeffrey glanced at Dana. "I'm sorry. Don't maim me."

She stared at him for what felt like forever before she snorted, turned, and began walking away.

He'd hoped his proclamation would have been Hollywood-movie worthy and that she'd fall into his arms. Not storm off.

It was evident he had some work to do in the leading man department.

Jeffrey made a move to rush after her and had to grab the shirt around his waist to keep it in place. "Legs, wait. Where are you going?"

"Back to the house," she said, her voice shaking somewhat. "I need a shower and to think. You need time to realize you're wrong about us."

"I don't need any time because I'm not wrong about us. And the house isn't in that direction," he said with a small laugh, hoping to lighten the mood. "You keep going that way and you'll end up at the Pickenses' farm."

She glanced at him, and the edges of her lips trembled. "Where is a squeaky toy when I need one, wolf-boy?"

It was an olive branch, and he was smart enough to take it.

"How about I walk you back, and on the way, we can play find my clothes," he said with a wink.

She gave a casual shrug. "Unless this involves you playing fetch, I'm not sure I'm interested."

"You can throw sticks and I'll retrieve them," he said, grinning more. "That should keep me busy and amuse you."

"Deal," she said.

Poppy cupped her mouth, her eyes growing moist. It was easy to see she was happy but trying to avoid bursting with joy and happy tears. It was a total Poppy thing to do.

"Brett, can you handle everything here?" asked Jeffrey.

"I've got this. Can you walk Marcy and Poppy back too?" asked Brett, kissing Poppy's temple quickly.

Jeffrey needed alone time with Dana but understood Brett wanting his mate away from the crime scene. "Of course."

"I want to stay. I can help put ghoul parts in bags," said Marcy. "Can I keep a few bits? Nothing important or anything. Maybe a foot or something."

Stratton's brows met. "You are very strange."

She smiled wide. "Thank you. You're handsome. Are you seeing anyone special?"

"Not at the moment," he said. "Would you like to have dinner with me?"

Marcy leaned against him, all smiles. "No. It will be weird when your mate gets here."

"I don't have a mate," said Stratton.

Marcy patted his forearm. "Sure, you don't."

"Jeffrey," said Brett. "Can you stay at the house

until I get back? I don't want the girls alone with everything that has happened. We don't know if Dragos will make another move on Dana. With Tuck being gone for who knows how long, I'd feel better if a man was there."

"Tucker is there," said Marcy. "He's a man."

"He's still in his teens," said Brett as if that didn't count.

"Didn't you tell me that your wife and her friends hit that succubus with a bolt of lightning and killed a bunch of evil thralled vampires?" asked Stratton.

"Yes," said Brett.

"And Dana took out a couple of these ghouls with relative ease," said Stratton. "Kind of like a slayer would."

Jeffrey tensed as more pieces fell into place. It all made sense. If they were right, and Abraham was part of the Van Helsing clan, and the same one mentioned in Stoker's story, he was a famed vampire hunter who just might actually be a vampire. And if he was Dana's father, it would mean she'd inherited the family destiny of policing supernaturals and possibly some of her father's vampire traits.

"Yes," said Brett. "Dana was pretty impressive with the vampires two nights ago too."

Stratton shrugged. "I don't know. Sounds like we should have the girls stay to protect us and be less worried about putting them in a bubble."

Dana laughed. "I like you."

Stratton smiled at Dana in a suggestive manner.

One Jeffrey didn't like in the least.

Jeffrey growled. "*Mine.*"

Dana groaned. "No. I'm not."

"Yes, you are," he returned.

She tossed her hands in the air and began ranting about not needing or wanting a man in her life. That he was a complication she didn't need and that he probably just wanted sex from her—nothing more.

Jeffrey only caught part of the rest of it because he was too busy staring at her sexy backside as she stormed off—in the wrong direction once again.

Stratton whistled, catching Jeffrey's attention.

Jeffrey glanced at him.

He held up a cell phone and nodded to Dana as she continued to rant and rave about how all men were bottom-feeding mouth breathers. "I think this is hers, and there is no way in hell I'm getting close to her right now."

Lifting a hand, Jeffrey waited as Stratton tossed the phone to him. He caught it, and the minute he did, the phone rang. He nearly dropped the thing.

"Dana," he said as her phone rang again.

She stopped shouting about men and spun around to face him. "What?"

Poppy laughed and wiped her eyes. "They're perfect for each other, Brett."

Brett licked his lips, as if trying to avoid laughing as well. "I think you might be right. She won't take any of his crap."

Jeffrey held up the phone, which displayed a contact that read "Nonna" as the phone continued to ring. "You've got a call."

Her brow creased. "I don't have service out here."

Jeffrey noticed that, technically, according to the bars on her phone, she still didn't have any coverage. But the phone continued to ring all the same. Boldly, he answered it. "Hello?"

"Are you the wolf?" asked a woman with an accent that sounded very Italian to him.

He stiffened, his gaze colliding with Dana's. "Yes. I'm the wolf."

"Is she harmed?" the woman asked, worry in her voice.

"Your granddaughter is fine," he said soothingly.

Dana hurried to him, her hand out for the phone.

"Hi, Wilma!" yelled Marcy, waving as she did, as if the woman could see her.

FIFTEEN

Dana

———————

I TOOK the phone from Jeffrey and brought it to my ear. "Nonna?"

She exhaled loudly, sounding relieved. "You're okay? I was worried."

"How did you know I was in trouble?" I tensed.

"I just knew," said Nonna. "I know a lot of things, but you tend not to believe me."

"About that." I sighed. "Nonna, are you really a witch? Like real magik and all of that?"

"Yes. You've got some witch in you too, Dana," said Nonna.

I did my best to remain calm. "What else do I have in me?"

She was quiet for a long while, and I knew I wasn't going to like the answer she provided.

"Nonna?"

"I knew this day would come," she whispered. "I feared it but knew it would come. The cards told me it was time to push you to return to Grimm Cove. That your wolf was there. But I knew the other was there too."

I swallowed hard. "Can you do me a favor and speak in clear terms? No riddles. And what do you mean by *returned* to Grimm Cove? I'd never been here before when you suggested I vacation in South Carolina."

A line of Italian curses came from Nonna as she asked for forgiveness for withholding the truth from me for so long.

I grunted. "Now who needs soap in their mouth?"

Nonna snorted. "I'm ninety. At my age, I can tell anyone anything I damn well please. I've logged my time and earned that right."

I rubbed my temple. "Nonna, please."

"Dana, you were born in Grimm Cove in secret and whisked off to New York—to me. It was the safest thing to do back then," she said.

"Safest? Why would I be in danger as a newborn? And why wouldn't anyone tell me I was born here? My birth certificate says New York."

She snorted. "I know a gal who knows a gal. In other words, I know people who get things done."

And just like that, I pictured her heading a crime family. She was small but mighty.

"Nonna," I said decisively, noticing Poppy easing closer to me. "How old was I when my father died?"

She grew quiet once more. "You weren't even born. You came after."

My gaze snapped to Jeffrey. Had he been right about Abraham being my father? "How long after he died was I born? A month? Two months? Nine months?"

"Yes," said Nonna.

I let my guard down. It was evident my father couldn't be the man they all thought he was. It was just a coincidence he had a similar name.

"Give or take a hundred years," she added quickly, as if it might go unnoticed.

"What?" I asked, paling.

Jeffrey came straight to me, the shirt around his waist falling some, revealing hipbone.

Marcy whistled loudly. "Hubba-hubba."

"Impressive," said Poppy.

Brett growled at him. "Stop putting on a show for my mate and her friends, Farkas."

"Like I meant to do it." Jeffrey grunted and readjusted the shirt before reaching for me. "Legs, are you okay?"

"Not really," I said, holding the phone out a bit. "Nonna said my father died a hundred years before I was born—give or take."

"I know," said Jeffrey before clearing his throat. "I can hear her side of the conversation. So can Brett. Shifter thing. I don't know what Stratton is, so I don't know if he heard it."

"I did," said Stratton evenly, offering nothing more on what he was or wasn't.

I found myself reaching out with my free hand for Jeffrey, needing comfort.

He grabbed my hand in his and drew me close.

I brought the phone back to my ear. "Nonna, I don't understand what you're saying."

"You do," said Nonna softly. "You just don't want to believe it's all true. There is an entire world of magik and the supernatural that your mother, your father, and I tried so hard to shield you from. I may not like him, but your father has always wanted you far from danger. He's lived a long time. And in that time, he's made a lot of enemies. If what my sources say is true, you met one of those enemies tonight—Dragos."

My mind raced to process what she was saying. In an instant, I thought about the night I'd seen my mother take on the rabid dog—that had looked a lot like a wolf. Before she'd done that, a mysterious man in a limo had pulled up and spoken with me, seeming concerned about my mother. As I focused more on that day, I realized where I'd heard Abraham's voice before.

It had been him—the man with the limo.

He'd also been at my mother's funeral, standing just outside of the church, looking in the open door at the service. He hadn't looked like he was over a hundred. Sure, it had been twenty years since I'd seen him, but still. He didn't look his age. In fact, he didn't look any older than me.

Someone had covered the full expense of my mother's hospital stay and her memorial service. Poppy and I had done our best to find out who that mysterious benefactor was, but we'd come up empty.

As my thoughts ran over my mother's expenses being paid for, another thing came to mind. My college education, and how at first my acceptance to Yale hadn't come with a full ride, but days later, I was granted a scholarship that more than covered all my needs.

Nonna and my mother's argument about too many strings being attached to my full ride made sense now.

"*He* paid for Yale, didn't he?" I asked, unsure I wanted to hear the answer.

"Yes," Nonna said, offering no more.

"Is he also the one who paid for Mom's funeral service and her hospital bills?" I asked.

"Yes," she said, hurt in her voice. "He is also the reason she died. Her feelings for him clouded her judgment when it came to other supernaturals, specifically vampires. Like her father, she found it in her heart to love a supernatural rather than destroy the ones who were beyond redemption."

"Grandpa was a hunter, as in slayer?" I asked.

"Yes. Many men prefer to be called hunters. And when he met me, he said he knew I was meant to be with him," she said. "I didn't think it was possible for a hunter and a witch to make a life together, but we did. It was a good one until he died. But I still had your mother then. She was a blessing. But she took after his side more than mine. It was her calling to be a slayer. Her destiny."

I thought about how easy killing the vampires and the ghouls had come to me. And about how I had no remorse over the act.

My blood ran cold. Was I a slayer too? "Nonna, do *I* take after his side too?"

She sighed. "Dana, your mother was half witch and half slayer. Your father was born a hunter—or slayer, if you prefer the term—but was turned into a creature of the night. That means you're—"

I gasped, clutching Jeffrey's hand tighter. "A quarter vampire, a quarter witch, and fifty percent slayer?"

"I was going to say a force to be reckoned with, but yes, if you prefer to do the math," said Nonna with a small laugh. "I'll let you go now and talk to you soon. I just needed to know you were okay. When Ellie-Sue and Tuck appeared to tell me they'd heard of an impending attack on you, I worried. And when the ether whispered to us that Dragos was behind the attack, we were all concerned."

I pressed myself against Jeffrey. "Are you telling me you talked to Poppy's dead grandparents?"

"Yes. Ellie-Sue and I go way back," said Nonna. "We met at a conference for witches when we were in our twenties. Over the years, we've helped one another whenever we could."

I just stood there, trying to let it all soak in. "Anything else I should know?"

"Yes," said Nonna.

I tensed, and Jeffrey moved his hand to my low back and rubbed it in a supportive manner. "I'm afraid to ask."

"You should know the animal you were born with a connection to is a wolf," said Nonna. "Just as your father has ties to wolves. And if I'm correct, you have a very special wolf standing there, wanting very much to hold you tightly but worried you'll snap at him if he tries."

I looked up at Jeffrey.

"She's right," said Jeffrey. "It was pointed out to me that you're very capable of ripping parts off me, and I'm standing here in Stratton's shirt. Hardly a cup or anything. Doesn't offer much in the way of protection."

I grunted.

Nonna laughed. "Tell him that I approve. And, Dana, I'm glad you're finally settling down with a man. That you'll have a family of your own. That you'll have someone with you when I'm gone. You won't be alone."

I stiffened. "Nonna, you're not planning to join Ellie-Sue anytime soon, are you?"

"I'm with her now," said Nonna.

I felt faint. "Is that how you got my phone to

ring without service here? You're dead and calling me from the other side?"

"Impressive calling distance," said Marcy.

"What? No. I'm calling you from the turnpike," said Nonna. "Peter is driving."

"I'm confused. You said you're with Ellie-Sue," I said. "I thought you meant you were dead."

"Oh, no. We're about to stop for gas."

I thought harder on it. "Peter is driving? A car? He's like a hundred."

"Hardly. He's a couple of years younger than me. I'm a cradle robber like that," she said proudly. "I think that means I'm a tiger."

Jeffrey snorted. "Cougar. She means cougar."

Nonna cleared her throat. "Rita and Lou say hi."

"They're with you too?" I asked, wondering what was going on.

She giggled softly, sounding so young. "Of course, they didn't want to miss out on an adventure. We're old. Not dead. George is here too. Chester as well. Not Shirley though. George and Chester bonded over how she treated them. We thought it best to avoid drama and leave her home."

"You've all managed to fit in one car?" I asked. "And fit Lou's oxygen tank machine in?"

"He has a portable one, Dana," she said as if I was being dramatic. "And we fit perfectly in the center's van."

I felt faint. "Peter is driving the van from the senior center?"

Jeffrey pried the phone from my hands. "Nonna?" He laughed. "Yes. I know she's not going to take kindly to me taking her phone. Thank you for your blessing. Yes. Of course I'll take good care of her. Well, no. We haven't discussed children yet. I sort of have to first convince her to go on a date with me. She keeps turning me down."

He tipped his head and locked gazes with me. "Dana, she said hold your head high. No walks of shame needed with me. Do I want to know what she means?"

"No," I groaned. "Find out why she and her cronies are in the senior center van. How did they get it? Did they steal it? Ohmygod, is Nonna breaking the law?"

Jeffrey laughed so hard, he teared up. "Nonna, I'm not going to tell her that. She scares me. Yes, ma'am. I will. And yes, I think I already am. I hope she gets on board with the idea. Ha. I'll be sure to tell her this isn't the first time you've broken the law."

Listening to the two bonding, I rolled my eyes. "Hang up before you hear about her sex life."

His eyes widened. "Bye, Nonna."

I took a look around at the aftermath of the ghoul attack and slumped my shoulders. "Is it always this way in Grimm Cove?"

Jeffrey glanced down at the ghoul nearest to us. "This is the first time I've ever actually seen ghouls in person. I've heard of them. And I think I remember my father mentioning having some run-ins with them when he was younger, but other than that, no."

"Same," said Brett. "This is my first time seeing them in the flesh too."

Everyone glanced at Stratton.

"I've seen more than my fair share," he supplied.

My throat went dry. "Since coming here, I've seen a lot of things I'd never seen before."

Jeffrey's posture stiffened. "Legs, I swear it's not always like this here. Something is in the air because we've had a lot of batshit-crazy things going on for the past six months. I want to lie and tell you it won't get worse here, but I can't make you that promise."

"Feels kind of like it's ramping up, doesn't it?" asked Brett. "Started six months back with the first succu-witch kill, and three months ago, those increased and we got into the brawl outside of your bar. That forced the council's hand on making changes. Around that time, other calls started coming into the station about strange things."

Stratton nodded. "Yep. And if we do have the legendary Dragos here, it stands to reason other really powerful baddies might be showing up."

A strange sensation came over me as I stared down at the ghouls. "Or they're already here, waiting for the right moment to strike."

"Could be," said Stratton.

"Can you not help?" Jeffrey growled at the man. "I'm trying my best to keep my mate from running back to New York."

Stratton gave him a thumbs-up. "Going great so far. Keep up the good work."

Jeffrey's attention went to Brett as he lifted a middle finger in Stratton's direction. "I'm going to eat your detective."

"Okay, but you're filing the paperwork when

you're done. Not me," said Brett with a grin. "You saw how I type."

With a nod of agreement, Jeffrey said, "You make it look awkward."

"As opposed to you wearing Stratton's shirt as a skirt?" goaded Brett.

I couldn't help but laugh.

SIXTEEN

Dana

———————

JEFFREY PUT his hand out to me as he stood there in nothing more than Stratton's shirt. "Come on, Legs. Let's find my clothes and get you back so you can shower. We can figure out the rest later."

I nodded.

He tugged on my hand and began to walk. Neither of us said a word for about ten minutes as I found myself lost in thought on everything I'd only just learned.

Everything I'd thought I'd known about myself and my life had been a lie.

Jeffrey pulled to a stop, and I jerked back to the here and now. He winked. "Sorry, but my pants are here."

It was then I noticed his discarded jeans on the ground.

Releasing his hand, I looked around for his underwear. "Did we pass your skivvies already?"

He licked his lips. "Nope. I don't wear them."

Interesting.

"And 'skivvies'?" he questioned with a snort.

I shrugged. "Nonna uses the word. It stuck."

He touched the shirt tied around his waist, and I realized I was staring at him. I'd have blushed, but I'd already seen him naked. Besides, he was hardly the first naked guy I'd seen in my forty years.

A sexy smile spread over his face. "Feeling bold?"

"Better question is, are you?" I countered.

With that, Jeffrey undid the shirt and let it drop to the ground.

That answered that question.

"Poppy, you're right. He *is* impressive," said Marcy from behind us, startling me.

I turned to find her and Poppy there.

Poppy waved as she tried to keep from laughing.

Jeffrey grabbed his jeans and hurried into them. "Shit."

Marcy beamed. "Don't let us stop you. Carry on with what you were both going to do—you know, each other."

"I agree."

I spun around at the sound of a woman's voice I didn't recognize.

There, standing off near a large tree, was an older woman dressed in a long, flowing, baby blue summer dress with matching slip-on shoes. Her curly hair was pushed back from her face with a blue checkered headband, drawing attention to her dark brown eyes.

Several other people stepped out of seemingly nowhere to join her.

I gasped. All of them had seen Jeffrey in the buff. They all appeared to be in their early sixties or above.

Additional people arrived, and I had to wonder if a mass email had gone out alerting everyone in the town that the local head of the wolf-shifters was in his birthday suit.

If there was such a mailing list, I really needed to sign up for it.

Jeffrey groaned and rubbed the bridge of his nose. "Maria, this isn't me getting into more trouble. I swear."

The woman lifted a dark brow. "Jeffrey, you know as well as I do that trouble just seems to follow you."

The people with her nodded. Several whispered amongst themselves about Jeffrey being a magnet for chaos. One man in particular snorted and nodded his head, stepping up more in the gathered crowd.

"You don't know the half of it," said the man, who looked to be in his early sixties. "You should have been around him daily when he was a toddler. The boy could make a preacher cuss, he got into so much trouble."

"Dad, you could take my side here," said Jeffrey. It was then I noted the similarities between the two.

The man had hair the same color as Jeffrey's but with more white through the sides. It was cut a bit shorter but just as full as his son's. His blue gaze was locked firmly on Jeffrey.

"Maria summoned the council. She said something dark and evil was out here. We show up and find you. Care to explain?" asked Jeffrey's father. He then noticed Poppy, and a huge smile spread over his face. "Poppy Proctor, or should I say Poppy Kasper?"

Poppy squealed and hurried toward the man, embracing him. "Mr. Farkas! I was meaning to get over and see you and Mrs. Farkas. It's just been a little crazy since I got back to town."

The man gave her a good hug and then stared down at her, seeming happy to see her. "So I hear. My son tells me Brett claimed you and that little ones are on the way."

Poppy blushed. "Yes, sir."

"It's about time that boy did right by you," said Mr. Farkas, his accent thicker than Jeffrey's even. "Wish he'd talk some sense into my boy. I've about given up on him settling down and mating. At this point, his mate would need to fall out of the sky and onto his head for him to take notice."

Maria eyed me. "Oh, I don't know about that, Jim. He might surprise you."

"Doubtful," said Jim as he crossed his arms over his chest, giving his son a disapproving look. "What are you doing out here barely dressed?"

"I shifted forms," said Jeffrey, glancing around at the forest floor. "I did it in mid-run, which means I stripped in mid-run too."

I spotted his T-shirt in a pile of leaves and hurried over to grab it. I held it up for him.

His gaze met mine as he approached. He took

the shirt, his hand wrapping around mine in the process. "Thanks, Legs."

"Guess that explains why one boot is over there," said his father, pointing just past me, "and the other is there."

"Uh, yeah," said Jeffrey, clearly uncomfortable with the attention.

Poppy stayed close to Mr. Farkas. "I need to stop by your place to see your wife and Jennifer."

Jeffrey tensed at the mention of the name Jennifer.

So did Mr. Farkas. "Faye would love to see you."

Poppy smiled wider. "Has Jennifer settled down and found someone yet? Are you and Faye grand-parents? Jeffrey hasn't given me the skinny on anyone in your family since I've been back."

"Well, Poppy, I'm not sure," said Jim. "Jennifer sort of left town a few years back and hasn't stayed in touch—with anyone."

Poppy shot Jeffrey a stern look. "And you never once thought to mention your sister wasn't in Grimm Cove and hasn't been contacting your family? Is she okay? Where is she? Do you know?"

Jeffrey shook his head. "No, but it's not for lack

of trying to find out. Last I saw her, she was high-tailing it out of town with a Van Helsing boy."

As he said it, his strong dislike of anyone named Van Helsing made more sense. He no doubt blamed the Van Helsings for the disappearance of his sister. "Jeffrey, I'm sorry."

He took a deep breath. "Not your fault, Legs. It's mine. I should have been more open to her dating a Van Helsing. It's just, well…slayers spent centuries hunting my kind. There is a lot of animosity there."

"I noticed," I returned.

"Doesn't help that the head of the slayers is a total asshole," added Jeffrey before glancing toward Maria. "Erm, a total pain in the butt."

Maria stepped forward, and something in her expression said she wasn't keen on the way the conversation was going. "I don't believe I've had the pleasure of meeting your friends, Poppy. These *are* your friends, correct?"

Poppy went to the woman. "Thank you for looking after the house for me."

The woman nodded. "It was my pleasure. Sorry I couldn't do more to get the bad energy out before you arrived. But it was a task for a Proctor witch."

"I understand," added Poppy.

Marcy shot forward and had her arms wrapped around Maria before anyone could think to stop her. She squeezed the woman, rocking her in place. "I'm so happy to finally meet you. I'm Marcy. I've heard so many good things about you. Most dead people around here are very fond of you. The animals love you too. A few flowers had some cross words for you, something about your familiar Slim. He's apparently been using their flowerbeds as a kitty litter stopping point, if you catch my drift."

Maria returned the hug and chuckled. "The wind whispered to me that you'd be coming back to us, Marcy. Happy to have you home now. Have you found Grimm Cove to your liking?"

"Oh yes!" exclaimed Marcy. "Very much so. It's kind of noisy here though with all the dead people, but that's okay. I'll never be lonely."

I just stood there, shaking my head. My crazy bestie had finally found her people. She fit right in. It was as if she'd happened upon the mothership of aura readers.

"Y'all okay?" asked Travis as he rushed onto the scene with other men in tow. From what I'd heard Travis was supposed to be resting, on the mend after being injured during the succu-witch attack, not running about in the woods.

I recognized a number of the people with him from two nights back. They'd arrived to help fight off the thralled vampires of the succu-witch.

"We're fine," said Poppy. "Why are you here and not at home healing?"

"I had the same question," I said.

"What happened?" asked Travis of Jeffrey, ignoring Poppy and me.

"That's what we'd like to know," said Jim, sounding annoyed.

Maria lifted a hand and Jim took a step back, giving Jeffrey some breathing room.

Seeing Jeffrey become the source of contention with everyone bothered me greatly. He'd done nothing wrong. Yet most of them looked at him as if he was the adult embodiment of Dennis the Menace. I half expected someone to shout at him to get off their lawn.

It was ridiculous.

"Some creepy dude named Dragos made a big section of the woods turn pitch black and then unleashed his ghoul minions on me," I said, drawing everyone's attention. "Jeffrey came to help *me*. Anyone who has issue with that can take it up with me personally. I, for one, am thankful he did."

Jeffrey glanced at me, his brows lifting.

Travis's jaw dropped. "Ghouls? We have ghouls now? I'm tendering my resignation."

Jeffrey grunted. "If only it were that simple. I'd hand in mine too."

"Ghouls?" echoed Jim. He looked to his son. "You're sure?"

Nodding, Jeffrey took a deep breath. "I'm positive. A whole mess of them. It's the rancid scent you're probably picking up on out here. Back that way is at least thirty dead ones. Brett and his detective are there, getting a cleanup effort going."

Maria's gaze swept to Jim and some of the others who had arrived with her. From their expressions, the news wasn't good.

Jeffrey edged closer to me as he pulled his shirt over his head. He was left standing there barefoot but dressed.

I darted over and retrieved his boots for him.

Travis helped with the second one, moving slow and favoring the side he'd been injured on. He handed the other boot to me.

I met his gaze and let mine go hard. "You should be healing. Not here."

"A wolf's gotta do what a wolf's gotta do," he said, falling back in line with the others.

I went to Jeffrey right away, holding his boots as he focused on his father. "There's more."

"It gets better?" asked Jim. "I'm almost afraid to find out how. Did you manage to get into a row with another group of supernaturals too? Seems to be your thing, son."

I didn't like seeing the way the people with Maria looked at Jeffrey as if he was a disappointment. I thrust his boots at him and stewed as he put them on, my irritation with the others, not him.

I found myself stepping up next to him and squaring my shoulders. "Would you rather he let me be attacked by smelly ghouls? I'm not sure what sort of character each of you has, but if it's the kind that runs from trouble rather than—"

Jeffrey grabbed for my hand once more. "Legs, stop. It's fine. I'm used to it. A lot is expected of me. I haven't exactly lived up to those expectations."

"Bullshit," I snapped, making Travis and the wolf-shifters he'd arrived with laugh.

Maria said nothing, but there was an odd satisfied look on her face as I set my sights on the people with her.

"I don't know what his duties entail, but if they include helping to stop a succu-witch, her evil vampires, and ghouls who are attacking a woman in the woods, then I'd say he's actually exceeding expectations," I said, my posture rigid as I fell back into prosecutor mode. "Tell me, who among you would have responded differently. I'd like an account of which of you would fail at being a good person."

Maria gave a slight nod before glancing at the others. "She makes a valid point."

Jim expelled an annoyed breath. "He should have summoned the pack for backup with the ghouls. He didn't. If he had, I'd have felt the call. Taking on a bunch of ghouls by himself was fool-ish. That's the kind of thing that gets an alpha killed and leaves his pack in disarray."

"He wasn't alone, Mr. Farkas," I said, cutting Jeffrey off before he could respond. "I was there, and I'm hardly chopped liver. And so were a bunch of slayers."

That caught Maria's attention. "Slayers were part of it all as well?"

"Yes. And they didn't come alone," said Jeffrey, sounding tired. "A man named Abraham was with them."

The group of people who had arrived with Maria all turned, forming a circle and talking amongst themselves.

I leaned in toward Jeffrey more. "What are they saying? Does your super-hearing pick up on it all?"

"Maria is a witch," he said in a hushed tone. "She can spell the area around her and the rest of the council so none of us can listen in."

"Council?" I asked.

"Group of Elders from each faction of species within Grimm Cove. Looks like most of them are here. A few are missing," he said, a smug look on his face.

"Why are you looking at me like that?" I asked.

He inclined his head. "Because you didn't question the bit about her being a witch and casting a silence spell. You asked about the council. I think that means you're getting used to Grimm Cove and its oddities."

He was right. I kind of was getting used to it all.

Not sure what that meant or said about me. I guess I'd found my people too.

"You okay?" asked Travis of me.

I nodded.

He looked to Jeffrey. "Jim is right, Jeffrey. You

should have summoned us all. Instead, I get a call from Brett, telling me something was going down out here and that you needed help. I called the rest of the pack."

Jeffrey inhaled deeply and nodded. "I know. But I had one worry on my mind, and it wasn't getting backup."

I tensed, understanding that worry he was talking about was me.

Travis stood silently watching the council members as they continued to talk in their special circle of silence.

After several long moments, Maria turned to face us. "You're sure the man who was with the slayers was named Abraham?"

Jeffrey nodded, giving my hand a small squeeze. "I'm sure."

Jim rubbed his jawline. "If he's back, that means we have trouble."

"Pretty sure this town had trouble *before* he got here." I bit my lip and cringed. "That was supposed to be an internal thought."

Jeffrey snorted. "That may be so, but you're not wrong, Legs."

Maria nodded. "Very true. But the arrival of

Abraham brings a whole new set of issues. He's the head of the slayers but he rarely, if ever, makes an appearance."

"I thought Elis was in charge," said Jeffrey.

"Even he has someone to answer to," said Maria. "Abraham—or Bram, as we know him—is that man."

I took a deep breath.

"Why am I only just hearing about this?" asked Jeffrey, sounding miffed.

"You didn't need to know about it before," returned Jim.

"Hold up—you people throw blame at Jeffrey about not doing his job correctly, but you only give him half the information he needs to do it?" I demanded.

"Legs, please stop. You're going to end up challenging everyone here," said Jeffrey.

I shot him a firm look.

He pursed his lips. "Carry on."

I nodded. "I intend to."

Travis grinned and elbowed the guy nearest him. "She's fierce."

"This is mild for her," said Poppy.

Marcy nodded. "It's true. She's not had coffee

yet this morning so really this could be far worse. Trust us."

Jim glanced at me and then inclined his head. "You're right. Jeffrey should have been given all the facts."

Jeffrey curled his hand tighter around mine for a second. "Legs, I'd like to put you on retainer."

I couldn't help but laugh slightly. "No need. I've got your back."

"Yes," he said, his heated gaze finding mine. "You do. And I've got yours."

Jim cleared his throat. "Son, if Bram is here, it could mean trouble for the pack. He's powerful and able to control wolves to a certain degree. Normally, he travels with shifters nearby. They're his eyes and ears during the daylight hours. They're loyal to him, not the pack."

Jeffrey focused on me. "The black wolf you saw."

"Makes sense, I guess. Well, as much sense as any of this can possibly make," I said.

"Maria, Harker always has the faint smell of a wolf on him. I thought it was because he has dogs or something," stated Jeffrey evenly. "It's not that, is it?"

Maria glanced at the other council members before shaking her head. "No. It's not because he has dogs, Jeffrey."

Jeffrey growled. "That asshat is a wolf-shifter, isn't he?"

Maria narrowed her gaze on him. "Language, young man."

"Sorry, ma'am, but I'm not wrong. He is an asshat," said Jeffrey, earning him a few laughs from the pack members and several of the council members.

Travis joined in. "I second that motion. Kellan is one."

I stiffened. "What did you say?"

Marcy smiled wide. "He said Kellan."

Poppy's brows met. "Dana, why is that name familiar?"

Marcy glanced at her. "Dana's grandmother told us about him once. Said he broke Dana's heart when she was in high school. Remember? He's the guy Dana never wants to discuss. The one who soured her to the idea of happily ever after."

"Broke her heart?" asked Jeffrey, his voice deepening. He let go of my hand quickly. "You had a thing with Kellan Harker?"

I ignored his outburst, looking to Maria instead. "Kellan is in Grimm Cove?"

She nodded.

I felt faint. "And he's a wolf-shifter?"

Again, she nodded.

Another thought occurred to me. "And he's one of the wolves Bram controls?"

"Yes," she said evenly.

I stared at Poppy and Marcy. "He didn't just *happen* to go to school with me, did he?"

Poppy sighed. "I don't know. My gut says no."

Marcy frowned. "Want me to get Brett and go for his kneecaps?"

Poppy leaned toward Marcy. "Pretty sure Dana can go for them all on her own with great effectiveness."

Jeffrey growled. "Answer me, Legs. You had a thing with Kellan?"

Slowly, I turned my head to look at him. "Excuse me, but did you just demand I answer you?"

He opened his mouth and then closed it fast, shaking his head. "Nope."

His father snorted. "Some alpha you're shaping up to be."

Maria eyed Jim. "Funny, didn't I see you

tucking tail when Faye was cross with you the other day?"

Jim tugged at his shirt collar. "No."

"Odd, I could have sworn I did," said Maria. "I'll call Faye later and ask about it."

Jim's eyes widened. "Fine. Yes. I bend quickly when she's upset with me."

"Casting stones then?" asked Maria.

Jim shook his head. "Not anymore."

Maria looked to be fighting a chuckle. She then coughed slightly. "Jeffrey, what all went on here? I'm told a lot of death occurred but that we lost none of our own. Is that right?"

"Yes," said Jeffrey.

"Things could have been handled differently," added Jim, earning him a sideways glance from Maria.

Jeffrey said nothing in his defense.

Turns out, he didn't have to. I did it for him. "If you want to blame someone, blame the buttmunch who goes by the name Dragos. Not Jeffrey. He didn't cause this. If anyone did, it's me. Dragos wanted to hurt me to teach Bram a lesson. Something about him interfering in a feud that wasn't his own," I said, refusing to let Jeffrey take the fall for something that wasn't his fault. He was only guilty of rushing in to keep me safe. Nothing more.

The council huddled again.

"Blue forty-two," I said, partially under my breath.

Jeffrey chortled. "Maria would be the quarter-back. For sure."

I snorted. "They all seem to look to her for guidance."

"She's the head of the council," he supplied.

Travis appeared antsy but remained in place, patiently waiting for the council members to finish talking to one another.

Marcy was bent near the base of a tree, touching something on the ground. I didn't want to know more. Whatever she was making friends with was keeping her occupied, and I was fine with that.

The council members broke the circle and formed a line. Maria stared at me. "Why would harming you teach Bram a lesson?"

I glanced at Jeffrey, and he nodded.

"Bram is allegedly my father," I said, still having a hard time believing it myself.

Maria stared at me...and her eyes grew moist. "Dana?"

I stiffened, wondering how it was she knew my

name. No one had told her yet, and I'd not formally introduced myself. "Uh, yes?"

"Look at you, all grown up now," she said, the edges of her lips curving upward. "The last I saw you, you were just hours old. I helped to wrap you up tight in a blanket and get you and your mother far from Grimm Cove. New York City was where you were both headed, if I'm right."

She'd been there when I was born? She'd known my mother?

Jeffrey squeezed my hand. "You all right, Legs?"

I nodded faintly.

Maria eyed our joined hands, and her smile widened. "Good. I thought *it* might be you."

"Thought what might be me?" I asked.

"The tornado force I had a vision of for Jeffrey's future," she said, as if that sort of thing was run-of-the-mill. "I got that same feeling when you were born. The air pressure in the room changed and it felt like controlled chaos. Best way I can describe it is the feeling in the air as a tornado is blowing in."

I stood there, holding Jeffrey's hand, unsure what to say. Though I had to admit that controlled chaos was probably the best description anyone had ever used for me. It was oddly fitting.

Jim nodded his head toward us. "Is it me or is my son looking awfully protective of her? And he's holding her hand. Not sure his mother would believe it unless she saw it for herself."

Maria smiled more. "It's not you. He's doing what feels natural, Jim."

Jim's brows shot up. "Are you saying she's his…?"

I huffed. "People, I'm not his anything. He's annoying, gets on my last nerve, hates anyone with my last name, and is entirely too arrogant for my liking."

Jeffrey lifted our joined hands and kissed my knuckles. "Aww, you say the sweetest things, Legs."

I couldn't help but laugh.

He drew me to him, dipped his head and pressed his lips to mine.

I didn't push him away. Instead, I returned the kiss—right up until I remembered having an audience. Then I stilled, my lips still against his.

He grinned. "I don't know if I should tell you this, but I think you have dried ghoul drool on your cheek."

I made a gagging sound.

Maria laughed. "Oh Dana, it's good to have you home as well. Soon enough, we'll have everyone back to where they belong—here in Grimm Cove. Poppy and Marcy, will you do us the honor of joining the council and me for some breakfast?"

Poppy looked to me. "I don't know. Dana, are you going to be okay? You just learned that Bram is your—"

I held up a hand, stopping her. "I'll be fine. Go ahead. I'll go back to the house and get cleaned up and check in on the twins."

"Travis, you and the other pack members can go lend Brett and Stratton a hand with ghoul cleanup," said Jeffrey, my hand still in his.

Maria grinned more, looking a bit sneaky in the process. "Jeffrey, aren't we closer to your cabin than the Proctor House, out this far?"

"Yes," he said.

"You should take her *there* to get a shower. The longer she has ghoul bits on her, the more likely she is to not be able to get the smell out," said Maria with a lick of her lips.

I yelped and tugged on Jeffrey's hand. "Take me home with you this instant!"

Jim laughed. "Poppy, how about we stop and

get the twins to join us all for breakfast? We'll pick up Faye as well."

"Okay, but you have to pry the kids out of their beds," she said with a shrug. "I'm not even sure getting to hear about ghouls will do the trick."

SEVENTEEN

Dana

———

I'M NOT sure what I was expecting Jeffrey's home to be like, but the stunning cabin, nestled partly in the woods, with one side open to the waterfront, wasn't it. The place was picture perfect, complete with a dock that had a boat tethered to the end and a small garden off to the side of the cabin. There was a shed that matched the cabin not far from the garden. Alongside the shed was a wooden table with a sink.

Jeffrey's hand found the small of my back. "That's where I clean any fish that I catch."

"You like to fish?" I asked, desperate to discuss anything *other* than my father and ghouls.

"I do," he said, caressing my back. "It's relaxing. When I'm out on the water I can forget about everything for a bit. If you want, I could take you with me next time I go."

I gave him a strained look. "I've never been on a fishing boat. I've been on a ferry before. Not the same thing. And I've never been fishing."

"Never?" he asked, seeming dismayed at the idea I'd missed out on the pastime.

"Never," I returned.

He shook his head. "Woman, we're going to have to change that as soon as we can."

I couldn't help but smile.

He took my hand in his as we walked down a cobblestone path that led to a wraparound porch on the front of the cabin. Two large wooden chairs were on the porch with a table between them. A red throw blanket was draped over the back of one of the chairs and a book sat on the table.

"You're reading *The Lord of the Rings*?" I asked.

He nodded. "It's a go-to comfort read for me. Too geeky for you?"

I laughed softly. "Are you kidding? I love it. I'm kind of a fantasy and sci-fi junkie. I think I might drive the girls crazy with it all. I make them have a yearly marathon with me where I force them to sit through *The Lord of the Rings* movies. Poppy normally falls asleep. Tucker likes them, so he's always excited when I pull them out. Pepper doesn't even try to pretend to be into them. One year I ordered us elf ears to wear while watching. Another year I bought us robes, staffs, and wizard hats. Marcy loved hers and wore it shopping twice."

"I can see her doing that." He chuckled as he led me up the stairs to the front door.

"I knitted her a Dr. Who scarf once," I admitted.

Surprise showed on his face. "You knit?"

"Poppy thought it would be a good idea to find hobbies we could do online over video conferencing with each other since we were spread out over the United States," I confessed. "She tried painting to start with but that was an epic failure for me. Marcy did great. Then it was cooking but Marcy went through a vegan stage around the same time, so we ended that quickly."

"And at some point, Poppy got around to knitting?" he asked, his lips curving upward.

I nodded. "Tucker and Pepper were little still so it was something she could do from the house. It took a bit for me to catch on but when I did, I excelled. At first, I was a very aggressive knitter. Everything was wound too tight."

He tipped his head back and swiped his hand over his mouth, clearly fighting a smile. "*You?* Aggressive? No."

"True story," I said, holding my head high. "I even made Tucker a Dr. Who scarf. He wore it nonstop for months. Didn't matter how warm it was in California."

"Bet Poppy loved that," he said with a waggle of his brows.

"Totally."

"So, you're close with Poppy's twins then?"

"Tucker and Pepper see me as an aunt and I see them as family too," I responded. "When they were little, I was at a loss with how to deal with them. Poppy's an expert with all that. Crotch goblins and I have a long-standing history of not gelling well. Pepper and Tucker seem to have been the exception."

He held the door open for me. "You never wanted any kids of your own then?"

I shrugged. "I honestly never gave it a ton of thought. My career was the most important thing to me, and I don't regret that. I'm incredibly proud of what I accomplished. That being said, I knew back in New York that I was ready for a change of pace. Never considered kids being part of that change though. My grandmother is always cramming the idea of starting a family down my throat. It's like she hasn't caught on to the fact that nothing should be left in my care. I can't even keep a houseplant alive."

"People have a way of surprising you," he said.

He slipped his boots off and I followed his lead, removing my running shoes just inside the doorway. I set them next to his boots and took a look around the huge great room.

"Jeffrey, your house is amazing," I said. "I think my entire apartment back in New York could fit in the living room area here alone."

"Come on, you can shower in the master bathroom," he said.

I lifted my arm and sniffed myself. "I smell like a locker room and a ghoul had a love child."

Jeffrey laughed and motioned for me to follow him.

I did.

"You smell like mint and citrus to me," he supplied.

"I smell like a mojito?"

He glanced back at me as he walked down a wide hallway. "Kind of, yes."

A frown touched my lips. "Don't tell Nonna.

She'll demand a re-sniff because they're not Italian."

Snickering, he stopped outside of an open door. "I'd love to meet her. She seems like a pistol."

"Oh, she's something all right," I said. "You should go with me when I head up to visit her."

He stilled.

I tensed. Had I just invited the man to go back to New York with me?

"I know, um, you're busy I'm sure with running the bar and the pack and stuff," I said quickly.

He stepped closer to me, invading my space, making my body heat. He dipped his head. "Legs, I'd *love* to go to New York with you to see your grandmother. I understand how important she is to you. If you want, I can toss her in the truck and bring her back with me. Might need to take backup. I've heard she's got connections."

I cackled to the point I teared up and then I began to cry. Except the tears weren't from being amused; they'd switched over to being ones that represented how overwhelmed I felt.

Jeffrey put a hand behind my neck and brought his forehead to mine. "I swear that it won't always be this way. Please don't give up on Grimm Cove."

I continued to cry, my hands bunching his T-shirt in the process.

"Don't give up on me…on us," he whispered.

In that moment, I didn't care how weak I looked, or how vulnerable I was. I sank against him and let him hold me as I closed my eyes.

He wrapped his arms around me, giving me the comfort I needed.

"My father is alive," I said softly.

"Kind of," he returned.

It was such an absurd statement, yet totally true and fitting, that I couldn't help but laugh through my tears. I ended up hiccupping and laughing harder over it all.

"Want something else to blow your mind?" he asked, rocking our bodies gently back and forth as he continued to hold me.

I nodded against his steely chest.

"In wolf form I *could* so lick my own butt," he said, a teasing note in his voice. "I haven't, but physically, it would be possible."

I roared with laughter to the point I barked.

Jeffrey laughed as well.

I drew back slightly from him and took a deep breath, gathering something close to control of myself. "Thanks for making me laugh. I needed that."

"Anytime, Legs," he returned. "How about I make you something to eat while you shower?"

I nodded, suddenly feeling very tired. The last forty-eight hours were catching up with me fast. "Sounds good. And thank you again, Jeffrey, for everything."

He winked and then led me into his room.

His bed was massive, and a pang of jealousy flared through me when I thought of all the women he'd probably entertained in it over the years. It wasn't as if I was a virgin and didn't have a sexual past. Yet it still bothered me.

Great. I'm now a jealous nitwit.

"Legs?" he asked, and I realized I'd come to a stop and was fixated on his bed. "You all right?"

"I have a mental image of you doing the dirty with a bunch of women in here. Suddenly, I'm jealous. I don't get jealous," I stated clearly. I was too old to bother making up an excuse for the way I felt.

He took a deep breath. "If it makes you feel better, I don't bring women back here. Mostly I go to their places."

"Oddly, that didn't help any, Jeffrey," I said calmly.

He took a deep breath. "Yeah, as the words were coming out of my mouth, I had a flash of the robot from *Lost in Space*. Danger, Will Robinson. Danger."

"Weirdly, you being able to yank that sci-fi quote out of the air makes it better," I said.

"Want me to talk endlessly about Star Wars? I can." He grinned widely.

I snorted. "Maybe another day."

"Like when I take you on our first date?" he asked, sounding hopeful.

I eyed him. "Or we could just skip the dating and do it."

He blinked in surprise. "You mean *it*, it?"

"How old are you? You can't say sex?"

"I can say it," he returned. "And do it. Oh man, can I do it."

"Good, because I think it sounds like the perfect way to forget about my morning," I said. "First, I need to shower. Then I will do with you as I may."

Jeffrey sighed. "I cannot believe I'm going to say this, but no. Not if you're going into it thinking you can put an emotional wall up between us. I don't want that, Dana. I mean, I do want to have sex with you—loads of sex—but I don't want it at the price of the connection I know we're forming."

I studied him for what felt like forever. "Have you been talking to Poppy and Marcy about how I am with men?"

He took an odd interest in the ceiling fan in his room as it spun around. When he began to whistle, I rolled my eyes.

"Let me guess, they gave you an earful about how I don't form emotional connections with men. I just sleep with them," I stated.

"Well, it wasn't put quite that way," he said, pushing his thumbs through his belt loops in the front of his jeans. He shrugged. "I'm out of my element here, Legs. I'm the same way normally. I sleep with women, but don't bother with anything more. I never wanted more from them. I want more from you. A hell of a lot more."

"Why? I'm cranky basically all the time. I only like a few people and the rest annoy me. I speak my mind. Twice a day I visualize throat punching someone, and I'm apparently the daughter of a vampire demon-slayer."

"Legs, if you think I missed the fact you can be…um, particular, you're wrong. Noticed that the minute I met you and you punched me in the face."

I groaned. "I didn't mean to do that."

He flashed a sexy smile. "I know. And I didn't mean to fall for you at the moment of impact, but I did."

He'd fallen for me?

Was he touched in the head?

Did he not hear all my faults?

With a chuckle, he moved to me quickly and stole a chaste kiss. "Legs, go shower. You're over-thinking it all. Just let it be."

"Does this mean we're not having sex when I'm done getting cleaned up?" I asked.

He stiffened and reached down, adjusting the front of his jeans. "Y-yes. That's what it means."

I licked my lower lip and he moaned. "If you say so. I'm going to go get naked now, rub soap all over myself, all while I'm wet."

"Evil, evil woman," he said, pointing to the master bathroom. "Off with you before I give in."

I laughed as I walked into it.

EIGHTEEN

Jeffrey

"I WANT to let her rest right now," said Jeffrey as he held his phone to his ear and paced out in front of his cabin.

"You're sure she's okay?" asked Poppy on the other end of the call. "And how did you manage to get her to take a nap? She's like a stubborn two-year-old when it comes to them."

He glanced at the door, knowing Dana was inside, on his bed, wrapped in a towel and nothing else. The temptation had left him out front, wearing the grass thin as he paced. He'd been doing as much for the past three hours.

Jeffrey had done his best to keep busy, making numerous phone calls for updates on Dragos. He'd even done laundry, seeing to it Dana's workout clothes were clean for when she woke.

"I refused to have sex with her," he said.

"I'm sorry, but what?" asked Poppy. "Did the legendary charmer of women just confess to me that he turned down sex with a hot woman? A woman I know for a fact he more than wants?"

"You heard it right," he said with a grunt.

She was quiet a second. "You fell for her fully already, didn't you?"

He opened his mouth to deny it and then sighed. "Yes."

"Part of that is because she's your mate, at least that's what Maria said while we were at breakfast," said Poppy.

Jeffrey nodded. "I get that, but the rest is just me."

"Good," she said. "And thank you for refusing to sleep with her while she's in a vulnerable position."

"Yeah, don't put me in for sainthood or anything. I really, really, really want to be with her that way," he said in a hushed tone. "More than I've ever wanted anything in my life."

Poppy laughed.

"I offered to feed her. When she was in the

shower, I went to the kitchen to make her a sandwich and get her a glass of sweet tea. When I got back, she was already out of the shower, sitting on the edge of my bed, wearing nothing but a towel, barely able to keep her eyes open. She nearly tipped right over. That was hours ago. She's been asleep ever since."

"Want Marcy and me to come over and help get her up and dressed?" asked Poppy. "Word to the wise, she's not very pleasant when she first gets up. Have coffee in hand if you dare approach her. Also, check her shoes for wildlife. Apparently, critters are drawn to her."

"Thanks. I'll remember that." He laughed softly. "I'm outside, keeping my distance and giving her privacy. And I have things under control here. I promise I'm taking good care of her. I eased her back onto the bed, making sure her towel stayed up, and then I covered her with a blanket. No funny business."

She scowled. "Jeffrey, I never thought for a minute you'd do anything that wasn't on the level with her like that. I just…I feel like I should be there for her. So much has happened in two days and to top it off, everything with her father has come to light."

He knew how close the women were. And he knew Poppy felt helpless. So did he at the moment. "I know. I promise that when she wakes up, I'll get her to eat something and have her call you to set your mind at ease."

"Do you love her?" she asked.

He was quiet for a moment before answering. "Yes. It's illogical, I know. I've only just met her, but I'm pretty sure I'm in love with her."

"Pretty sure?" asked Poppy, sounding as if she was amused.

He snorted. "Okay, really sure."

"Good," said Poppy. "Jeffrey?"

"Yes?"

"I'm glad you're her mate," she said before she disconnected the call.

He stood there, holding his phone in hand, still trying to get his scattered thoughts to align. It was hard considering the fact the smell of Dana was everywhere now. He wanted to crawl into the bed next to her and bask in the glory of her scent, covering himself in it as well as getting his own on her.

It was a shifter thing. One he'd heard his father and Brett's dad discussing once long ago. Apparently, it was normal for a male shifter to want to have his scent on his mate and have hers surrounding him at all times. Jeffrey had always thought that was ridiculous and that something so insane could never happen to him—yet here he was, ready to roll in sheets just to smell like the woman he craved.

His wolf had been making itself known for the past hour of his pacing, wanting him to go back inside and claim his mate. Explaining to the beast that the woman could geld it wasn't an option.

It didn't care.

Clearly, it lacked a keen sense of self-preservation.

Dana really would can his balls if he tried claiming her at the moment.

Not the time, he thought as he continued to pace.

He needed to focus on Dragos. So far, he'd reached out to Brett four times only to be told no one had any information on the demon. At least none they were willing to share.

The slayers had closed ranks and weren't talking to anyone.

The only good thing that had come out of his endless calls was that he learned the dead ghouls had been removed from the woods and disposed of properly.

He needed more information. It was the key to keeping his mate safe.

Jeffrey scrolled through his phone until he found Elis's contact. It was labeled "Elis Van Douchebag."

He cringed, realizing he'd need to edit that later to avoid issues with Dana.

His thumb hovered above the call option.

Elis hated him and wouldn't answer his call.

The only reason Jeffrey even had the man's number in his contacts was because Maria had insisted all the men in charge exchange information.

As Jeffrey stood there, debating on calling a man he despised, his thoughts ran to Jennifer.

Had he missed the signs of his sister finding her mate? Could it be that Chad Van Helsing, the guy she'd run off with, was the man who had been made for her?

Closing his eyes, Jeffrey did his best to stop the building pressure in his chest as guilt filled him. It was impossible to wrap his mind around someone telling him he couldn't see Dana again—that he had to abandon the idea of more with her and let her go.

He'd only known the woman two days and

already he was willing to sacrifice everything for her. If his sister had found her true mate, it would have explained why she ran away with him and didn't look back. And it was high time Jeffrey thought about letting go of some of the anger he held toward Elis and the other slayers.

He stared down at his phone and gave in, pushing the call button. He assumed Elis would either ignore it or send it to voicemail.

When he answered, Jeffrey was so surprised that he didn't speak.

Elis groaned. "Dickhead, I know it's you. Crank calls are so thirty years ago."

"Bite me," snapped Jeffrey.

"That's your department, wolf," returned Elis. "What do you want?"

"Information on Dragos," said Jeffrey, lowering his voice as if someone might overhear the conversation. "And details on Abraham Van Helsing."

"Because you think it will give you the upper hand in the long-standing feud our kinds have had, or for another reason?" questioned Elis, his voice changing slightly—sounding less annoyed.

Sighing, Jeffrey let go of his hate of the man at least temporarily. "For Dana. I need to know how to keep her safe. That means I need to know exactly what I'm dealing with."

"What's your interest in her?" asked Elis. "Because if you think for one second Bram is going to let her be another notch on your bedpost—"

"She's my mate, Elis," said Jeffrey, waiting for a smart-ass remark.

None came.

"You're sure?" asked Elis.

"Yes."

Silence spread between them for a couple of minutes.

"Dragos is bad news, Jeffrey," said Elis finally. "He's old. Really old."

"Is he a vampire?" questioned Jeffrey.

"Yes and no," supplied Elis, his vagueness annoying. "He's a lot like one but his extra gift is the ability to summon other demons—bottom-feeders."

"Like ghouls?"

"*Exactly* like ghouls," answered Elis. "He doesn't like to get his hands dirty, but he will if he has to. He's powerful and strong. We think he's not a hundred percent just yet, but close. When he's at full strength, I'm not sure we'll be able to stop him."

"We?"

Elis exhaled loudly. "The slayers. Bram, specifically. Am I to assume you know about his connection to your mate?"

"That he's her father?" asked Jeffrey.

"Yes," replied Elis, confirming the news.

"Why has he stayed hidden from all of us and her?" demanded Jeffrey.

"Because a lot of folks have a hard time wrapping their minds around the fact the head of the slayers is a creature of the night," said Elis. "And he let Dana believe he was dead in hopes it would keep her safe."

"Well, that went great, didn't it?" asked Jeffrey coldly.

Elis grunted. "Listen, if you tell anyone else this, I'll deny it, but *I* didn't even know about her. Bram kept her existence a secret from nearly *all* of us. And if you think that in some way implies that he doesn't love her or care about her, you'd be wrong. Dead wrong. I've fought by his side before and let me tell you, his response when he learned Dragos was going for Dana was like nothing I've seen from him before. He lost his shit, Jeffrey."

"How *did* he find out about the attack?" asked Jeffrey.

Elis fell silent once more.

"Harker?" prompted Jeffrey. "Is he linked mentally with Bram?"

Jeffrey had never experienced anything like that but had heard tales of shifters who were bound to master vampires. They could link mentally, something vampires could do amongst themselves.

"Yes. All the Harker wolves are," answered Elis.

"And Bram had Kellan watching over *my* mate?" asked Jeffrey, his anger rising.

"No," said Elis, a certain level of exhaustion evident in his voice. "Bram didn't know Dana was in Grimm Cove. His people in New York didn't realize she'd come this way either. News of the succu-witch attack drew Bram's attention. He'd been out of the country at the time. He just got back right before word of Dragos going after Dana reached him."

"You expect me to believe Kellan just happened to be in the woods at the same time Dana was about to be attacked? I know they dated in high school. Is he wanting something more from her?" asked Jeffrey, not buying the story for a minute.

"I expect you to believe it, because it's the truth," said Elis. "He's been having some issues with his wolf side. I told him to ask you about it, but he'd rather get a paw stuck in a hunting trap than admit to you he needs help. Can't say I blame him. You're a total dick."

Jeffrey rubbed the bridge of his nose. As much as he disliked Kellan, he couldn't turn his back on a fellow shifter in need. "What kind of trouble is he having with his wolf?"

"It's been on edge for weeks," confessed Elis. "I thought the succu-witch's power might have been influencing him somehow, making his wolf cagey, but that would have ended with her death."

Jeffrey's posture went rigid. "Could Dragos's presence be affecting Kellan's wolf side? If his line of wolves is tied to vampires, it stands to reason that another master vampire could influence his wolf to some degree."

"Shit," breathed Elis. "Bram is an offshoot of Dragos's line of vampires. That means Dragos's dark power *could* be influencing Kellan in a negative way. It would explain why he's been off his game lately. And why he's been spending so much time patrolling the woods in wolf form. He must be sensing something out there—maybe even Dragos himself."

"It really was blind luck that he was out there

when my mate needed help, wasn't it?" asked Jeffrey, already knowing the answer.

"Yes. You better pucker up and kiss Fate's backside, Farkas," said Elis. "You owe it one."

"You might be right."

Elis was quiet a moment. "Jeffrey, Kellan was hurt trying to protect Dana. He managed to link with Bram long enough to call for help, but then things got ugly for him."

"How hurt is he?" asked Jeffrey, genuinely concerned. The man had done his part to keep Dana from being seriously injured or killed by Dragos and his minions. Jeffrey didn't want to see him hurt.

"I just left the clinic," returned Elis. "It's not looking great."

"I'm sorry to hear that," said Jeffrey before clearing his throat. "What can I do?"

"Can you spare some guys to guard the clinic? I don't want Dragos getting any ideas in his head about using Kellan for anything," added Elis. "And my slayers are spread thin, hunting for Dragos."

"You got it," said Jeffrey. "Is Austin all right?"

"He's fine. He'll be touched to know you asked," said Elis in a teasing tone.

"Yeah, well, I put a lot of time and effort into training him to run the bar. Wouldn't want to see that go to waste." Jeffrey snorted. "And now that I know he's kin to Dana, and not trying to put the moves on her, I find myself liking him more than I did."

Elis chuckled but it sounded forced.

"What aren't you telling me?" asked Jeffrey.

With a sigh, Elis said, "Dragos may win this one, Jeffrey. Bram is the only person I know who stands a chance against a demon as old as the one in Dragos. He could have wiped the floor with the rest of us. And the ghouls he summoned, they were organized and stronger than others I've run into in the past."

"Great. He's got them hopped up on Dragos-juice or something," added Jeffrey. "The day keeps getting better and better."

"Do you have eyes on Dana?" asked Elis.

"She's here, at my cabin. I don't plan to let her out of my sight. That going to be an issue with Bram?" questioned Jeffrey.

"From the little I was able to gather about Kellan and how it is he knew about Dana when I didn't, he might. I guess Bram sent Kellan and his parents to New York years ago with the idea his parents would help watch over Dana, her mother, and another woman," said Elis.

"Her grandmother, is my guess." Jeffrey scratched the back of his neck. "Let me guess, Bram had Kellan enrolled at the same school as Dana so a slayer would be close to her at all times."

"Sounds like it," replied Elis. "A slayer who also shares his body with a wolf. That makes Kellan pretty damn powerful. But when Bram learned the pair were dating, it sounds like he didn't take it well and yanked Kellan and his family out of New York faster than green grass through a goose."

Jeffrey hated hearing about Kellan and Dana being a couple, but he needed all the facts. Knowledge was power. The more he was armed with, the better chance he'd have against the enemy.

"I got this information from Kellan's mom. She's at the clinic, waiting as they operate on him," said Elis. "She told me that Bram didn't even let Kellan say good-bye to Dana when he forced them to leave New York. He ordered them back to Grimm Cove and forbid Kellan from reaching out to contact Dana. That means she never got an explanation as to why he left—only the knowledge that he left. Also means I wouldn't want to be you when he hears you're his daughter's mate. Nice knowing you, Farkas."

Jeffrey worried his jaw. "Something is bothering me. How is it Dragos and Bram could be out in the daylight? I thought all vampires had to avoid it."

"The really old ones can tolerate indirect light for certain lengths. And some, like Dragos and Bram, can create darkness," answered Elis.

"So they could attack someone at any time, in any place?"

"Yes, in theory, if they really wanted to," replied Elis. "I've told you more than Bram is going to be happy about, I'm sure. If I'm lucky, he won't kill me for opening my big mouth."

"Why *are* you helping me? You hate me," asked Jeffrey.

"Because my gut says having you owe me one is worth its weight in gold and that I'll need to cash in on that favor in the near future," said Elis. With that, the man hung up.

NINETEEN

Jeffrey

———————

FEELING as if the weight of the world was on his shoulders, Jeffrey took a second to regroup and gather his thoughts before making any more calls. What he really wanted to do was hunt down Dragos and end him, eliminating the threat to Dana. But he couldn't leave her unprotected.

He wouldn't.

He swallowed down a lump in his throat and called Brett.

"Farkas, I have no more leads than the last time you called," said Brett, obviously annoyed. "I'm following up on something right now. It's more than likely nothing, but Stratton is coming with me just in case. Travis is back at the house with Poppy, Marcy, Pepper, and Tucker. I didn't want to leave

Travis with them, seeing as how last time I did, it went *so* great, but I trust him. Plus, my wife scares me and threatened to maim me if I didn't give her some space, so I sort of got when the getting was good."

"I have new information," stated Jeffrey.

"I'm all ears," returned Brett.

Jeffrey filled him in on everything he'd learned from Elis.

"Not sure how I feel knowing ancient vamps can basically come and go as they please, to hell with daylight," said Brett.

"Yeah, my thoughts exactly."

Brett cleared his throat. "Elis really thinks Dragos could win this?"

"Yes."

Elis was a tool, but he was battle-tested and had been in the game the same length of time as Jeffrey and Brett. If he was worried, there was a major cause for concern.

"Do you?"

"Over my dead body," snarled Jeffrey.

"That's precisely what I'm afraid of."

Jeffrey rotated his shoulders, needing to work the stress and tension out of them. "Brett, if I fall in battle protecting the people we care about, I'm fine with that."

"I'm not," said Brett. "Who else will put up with me?"

"Good point. I'll try to stay alive."

"Thanks."

"Hey, send a detail to the clinic to watch over Kellan and his family," added Jeffrey. "I promised Elis I'd see it was done."

"I'll handle it. You okay with this whole Kellan and Dana thing?" asked Brett.

"No, but I don't want the guy dead over it," returned Jeffrey.

"I'll send men over that way. Do me a favor and don't do anything stupid between now and when I see you again," said Brett.

"No promises." He snorted and hung up.

Jeffrey stared out at the water, wondering what kind of favor Elis might need from him. Whatever it was, he'd do it. Dana meant that much to him.

Tipping his head, Jeffrey tapped into his shifter hearing and listened for the sound of her breathing. He'd been doing as much every five to ten minutes since she'd fallen asleep. An irrational fear that she'd stop breathing in her sleep filled him.

He shoved his cell in his back jeans pocket and ran his hand through his hair.

"Think of something other than having her in your bed right now," he said out loud.

All that did was make him think of how her long dark hair had looked against his white sheets. It had fanned out around her. Her skin was flawless. He'd wanted to touch her but didn't dare. He'd screamed in his head that "she was lava" and reverted to a child's game of avoiding being burned by staying clear of said lava.

Whatever works.

As he glanced down at the front of his jeans, he knew just how much the plan wasn't working. He'd basically had a hard-on for just over three hours. He'd need to seek medical attention soon.

With a groan, he adjusted himself and made the bold (or totally boneheaded, he wasn't sure just yet) decision to head back inside. He'd shower and then check on Dana again.

The minute he set foot in the house, he heard her whimper.

His cabin was sizeable, but he covered the distance in record time as he raced to the master bedroom. When he got there, he found Dana on the bed, still asleep. She whimpered again and shook her head slightly. It was then he realized she was having a bad dream.

His bare feet padded across the wood floor on his way to her. When he got to the side of the bed, he reached out tentatively and brushed a strand of dark hair from her cheek. "Legs, you're dreaming."

One second he was standing next to the bed, and the next he was flat on his back, on the floor, with Dana straddling his waist, pinning his arms out to each side.

Yep. She's got slayer in her.

He'd have laughed at the situation, but he realized that she was now minus the towel. His erection reached a point that it was painful. "Dana."

She blinked, appearing confused before she glanced around the room, then down at him. "Jeffrey?"

He bit his lower lip, fighting the urge to move his hips under her. "Yes?"

"Why are you on the floor?" she asked, seeming confused.

"Because you just pinned me to it," he replied, trying to appear unaffected.

She wiggled on him and he sucked in a big breath, going ramrod stiff. She glanced down at herself and gasped, sitting up straight on him, her arm going over her breasts. "I showered and then I…I fell asleep."

He nodded, closing his eyes, trying to think of anything but the fact the hottest woman he'd ever seen—the woman who was created for him—was naked on top of him.

"Why are your eyes closed?" she asked.

He peeked out of one. "Trying to give you privacy."

She snorted, lowering her arm from her breasts slightly. "Thanks, but I don't think I have anything you haven't seen before."

His hips, tired of listening to his head, moved on their own.

Dana stilled above him and then grinned, her hands finding his T-shirt. "Impressive is right."

He thumped his head on the floor twice, hoping it would knock sense into him. It didn't. "Dana, please. We should get up unless you're fine with me—"

She bent, her face suddenly near his. Their gazes locked as she put her lips closer to his. "I'm fine with it."

"Seriously?" he asked, his voice rising in pitch.

"Can I interest you in playing stuff the cannoli?" she asked.

"If that means what I think it does, hell yes!" His hands found her hips.

She grabbed his wrists and pinned his arms out again. "Stay."

He snorted. "Fine, but I'm not fetching shit right now."

She grinned as she put her lips near his once more. When she kissed him, he thought for sure he'd lose control and finish before he even got started. She teased his mouth with hers before her tongue skimmed over his lower lip.

The wolf within him roared with need and nearly overtook him. He held on by a thread as his eyes burned with the change. He knew they were now icy blue, but he couldn't help it. His emotions were too heightened.

Dana locked gazes with him and then kissed him full on, grinding her body against his.

He devoured her mouth, wanting more from her.

She bit at his lower lip and tugged on it with her teeth.

The act sent his shifter side into a frenzy. The next he knew, he'd taken the lead, flipping her over onto the floor, putting him on top. He went at her mouth as she grabbed his upper arms, then quickly moved to trying to get his shirt off.

Jeffrey broke the kiss long enough to yank his T-shirt over his head and cast it aside. He then returned to kissing Dana.

She ran her hands down his sides, scratching at his skin lightly, but enough to excite his wolf even more. Not that it needed any assistance. It was doing just fine in the horny department.

She made her way to the button of his jeans in no time, undoing it quickly.

He bit at *her* lip this time, growling as he did.

Dana jerked open his jeans and freed his erection. She stroked him and he almost exploded in her hand.

Jeffrey reached down and took over, lining up with her heated core. She was wet already, and he paused the kiss.

"What in the hell are you waiting for, Farkas?" she snapped. "A written invitation? Get a move on it. Now."

"Yes, ma'am," he said, driving into paradise.

For a second, everything around him felt as if someone had set off a bomb in his room. There was a swirl of wind that came out of nowhere. Pressure knocked into him as he pumped in and out of her tight body. As quickly as it started, the wind stopped, but he didn't. No. He kept going, kept thrusting as pleasure built deep within. He had to wonder if he'd imagined the wind because nothing was out of place in his room.

Dana moaned against his mouth, her eyes closed tightly, her legs wrapping around his waist. She managed to artfully work his jeans down more with her legs and feet and then she slapped his backside with both hands. "Harder."

He obliged.

She cried out below him, her body tightening around his.

He slammed into her, rooting deep, his gums burning with a pending shift. The feral need to mark her was all-consuming. He turned his head, trying to hide it from Dana. All he wanted to do was bury his face against her neck and sink his teeth into her flesh.

She grabbed the sides of his face and lifted her head, kissing him thoroughly.

His incisors lengthened, and she nicked her tongue on one. Blood filled his mouth and he swallowed it down, his entire body straining as he began to pump in and out of her once more, expelling his seed in process, deep within her.

She cried out and clung to him as he tipped his head back, fighting a full shift.

Never had he felt this much pleasure.

"Mine," he growled out, still in her, the taste of her blood running down his throat.

Dana grunted under him. "No, I'm not."

"Yes, you are," he said, the alpha in him rising quickly.

She arched a dark brow.

He cringed. "Uh, if you're okay with the idea."

Her lips twitched and she narrowed her gaze on him. "I'm warming to it."

That was something.

She stared up at him with an odd expression on her face.

He didn't pull out.

She ran her hands over his upper chest. "Is this a claiming?"

Jeffrey stiffened but nodded. "Well, it was. You shut it down."

"No, I didn't," she argued.

"Yes, you did." He realized she liked to be difficult just for the sake of being difficult. A sly grin spread over his face as he kicked off his jeans. "It's best you not claim me back. In fact, don't."

"I can claim you if I want to," she returned.

"No, you can't," he said, fighting the urge to laugh. She was so stubborn that she was downright predictable. He was about to withdraw when Dana grabbed his butt and jerked him against her harder.

"Mine," she said.

His eyes widened as it suddenly felt as if he'd slipped his skin for a second, seeing himself through her eyes. It felt as if nature was weaving threads between them, forming an unbreakable bond.

His hips began moving of their own accord and let his wolf rise a bit more, giving into his baser needs, thrusting into his mate, riding her and the wave of pleasure to its fullest.

He roared as she cried out, the two of them reaching culmination together. He shuddered, feeling complete and totally tied to the woman below him—his wife.

A slow grin splayed over his face as he stared lazily down at her. "I thought I told you not to claim me."

"Shut up, Farkas," she said, sticking her tongue out at him. "You don't tell me what I can and can't do. You're not the boss of me."

"Noted."

TWENTY

Dana

———————

"WHAT'S ALL OF THIS?" I asked, coming out of the bedroom to find Jeffrey at the center island in the great room.

Containers of food were all over the counter and everything smelled delicious.

He was in a different pair of jeans, without a shirt or shoes as he stirred a pitcher of what appeared to be iced tea. He presented a picture so tempting, I nearly rushed him and had my way with him again. It wasn't as if I hadn't done the same thing four times already today. I was nothing if not a master of avoidance, and I was doing some serious avoiding when it came to discussing the events of the morning and the revelations they'd brought about.

Jeffrey's hair was still damp from the shower we'd shared. I was in my running clothes again because they were the only things I had with me. Since he'd been nice enough to wash the ghoul bits off them, they no longer smelled like a locker room and a ghoul had a love child.

He pouted when he saw me. "I was hoping you'd decide to stay naked."

"I would but we don't seem to get far from the bedroom then," I said, nodding to his jeans. "*You* have on clothes."

"Only because my mother and father were here a little bit ago," he returned, setting the pitcher on the island and then grabbing two glasses. He filled them with ice and set one in front of me. He then set about pouring tea for me. "They brought over food. Enough to feed an army. I hope you're hungry."

"This is all for just us?" I asked, staring at the buffet before us. It looked to be enough to feed ten.

He patted his rock-hard abs. "I worked up an appetite. Besides, Momma tends to cook when she's excited or anxious. Since she's feeling better today, and my dad told her about you, she had a lot of nervous energy. It all went into cooking and baking."

His mother had managed to make everything before us in just a day? Impressive. Nonna would even tip her hat to Mrs. Farkas.

"I didn't hear them arrive or I'd have come out to see them," I said. "Jim and I get along *stellar*."

Jeffrey laughed. "Thank you for defending me to my father. But you don't have to do that."

"Yes I do," I countered. "Is your mother like him? Does she think you could be doing things better?"

"Her number one issue with me has been my romantic life. She's been at me to get out and find my mate for years now."

I wisely stayed quiet on the topic of mates, letting him speak instead.

His lips curved into a smile. "She's pretty darn happy I'm off the market now and she can't wait to meet you. I had to physically block her path to the bedroom, or she'd have charged in while you were finishing up in the bathroom."

"Thanks. I want to meet her, but I'd rather be dressed for it," I said.

He chuckled. "I tried to tell her you were sleeping but she wasn't buying it. She might have sort of guessed what we've spent our day doing."

"Fighting ghouls?" I asked with a smirk.

He tipped his head. "*And* going at it like bunnies."

"Interesting animal choice there, wolf-boy," I said. Then I thought more about his mother knowing what we'd been up to. As free as I was with my sexuality, I wanted his mother to like me. "She probably thinks the worst of me. I jumped into bed with her son after only knowing him forty-eight hours."

Longer than some of the men I've been with.

I kept that bit to myself.

Jeffrey shook his head. "She was thrilled to know the deed had been done and that I claimed you. Her exact words to me were for me to 'focus on blue.'"

Confused, my forehead creased a second before I caught on to what she'd meant. "She wants grandchildren? From me?"

Jeffrey bit his lip and nodded.

My eyes widened. "Did you tell her I can't keep a plant alive?"

"Nope. Tradition in the Farkas family has all the firstborn sons taking over the pack when they're older."

I began to walk back and forth in his kitchen as

he continued to hold a glass of iced tea for me. "This is bad. Really bad. Call her and explain how not-nurturing I am. Hurry before she pins her hopes on me."

He leaned back against the counter as I spun out of control.

"What would I do with a crotch goblin?" I asked, more to myself than him. "I mean, besides forget to water it."

"Pretty sure that's not how it works, Legs," he said, oddly calm about the entire ordeal.

I spun to face him. "Did you tell her I threatened Marcy's familiar with a shoe? It's proof that I'm a horrible person."

He had the audacity to laugh at me.

"Be serious here a minute!"

He set the tea on the counter and came to me. He took hold of my upper arms and drew me closer to him. "Oh, I'm taking this *very* seriously."

"Hardly. You're laughing at me."

"Legs, you're being ridiculous," he said in a low tone. "How about we just focus on the here and now and not what may come?"

"So you agree I shouldn't be allowed to nurture anything?" I asked.

"What answer is going to make you be less worked up right now?"

I cupped his scruffy cheeks. "Jeffrey."

"Dana," he returned, waggling his brows playfully. He then dipped his head and inhaled deeply near my neck. "Mmm, let's skip the food and go straight to the bedroom for dessert."

"Why do I get the feeling you're trying to hold me at your house?" I asked.

He stilled.

I eased back from him. "You *are* trying to keep me here, aren't you? Jeffrey, you can't hide me forever from Dragos. And at some point, I need to face my father. He's got some explaining to do."

"I know, but for now, can we let this be enough?" he asked. "Please. Just a bit longer."

Evidently, he was going to give me a race for my money in the avoidance department.

Sighing, I conceded and sat on one of the stools at the center island.

He seemed content as he grabbed the tea that he'd poured for me. He handed it to me.

Taking a sip, I expected it to taste like iced tea did back in New York. I was not anticipating the mouthful of syrupy sweet liquid I got. In an instant, I was darting to the sink, spitting it out. "Way to nearly take me out with sugar, Jeffrey. Save Dragos the time."

He was quiet and I turned to see him staring at me with wide eyes. "You don't like sweet tea? How can that be? It's a staple. I'm pretty sure it's one of the food groups in the South."

"I could stick my head in a bag of sugar and somehow get less sugar than I just did," I disputed.

He shook his head, disappointment evident. He mumbled something about Yankees and then got me a glass of ice water.

I sipped it, trying my best to get the taste of the tea from my mouth. "That stuff is foul."

He bent near me, stealing a fast kiss as he did. "You're just lucky I love you or those would be fighting words, Legs."

I went perfectly still, unsure what to say or do with what he'd just said.

"Legs?"

I focused on my feet.

He cupped my face and I set the glass of water on the counter behind me, still looking down.

"This is a lot for you," he said. "All of it. I know. Me saying what I did freaked you out, didn't it?"

It did and it didn't. What freaked me out the

most was how strong my emotional response was to him. It was a foreign feeling to me.

"Legs, would it help to know I didn't mean to say it out loud?" he asked, his tone light.

A small laugh bubbled up from me as my hands went over his on my face. I met his gaze. "Yes. It helps."

"You do realize we're husband and wife now as far as supernaturals are concerned, right?" he asked and bent more as I tried to duck away. He didn't let me. "I'm on a roll here so I'm getting all the big things out of the way."

"I'm going to require baby steps," I confessed.

"Bit late for that, Legs," he said.

He was right.

I took a deep breath and nodded. "I can do this. I can be a wife."

"Are you trying to convince me or yourself?" he asked, fighting a laugh.

"Me, at least I think me," I returned. "This will just take me a bit to get used to. You're right. Everything that has happened has been a lot to deal with."

He kissed me tenderly before putting his nose to mine. "After we eat, I could run outside and track dirt in all over the house. Would that make you feel better?"

Confused, I tipped my head slightly. "What?"

He winked. "Poppy said you clean when you're worked up. I could make a mess, so you have something to focus on."

"That is the nicest thing anyone has ever offered to do for me," I said, my mood improving quickly. As my stomach rumbled, my gaze went to the food. His mother's spread looked delicious. "We should feed me."

He motioned to the food. "Dig in. Momma wasn't sure what you liked so she made too many options to list."

I glanced at him and arched a brow. "Ordering a pizza would have been fine by me."

"Marry me," he said with a sexy grin.

"I already did that—at least that's what I've been told."

He swatted my backside in a playful manner. "How about we do it in a church? Would that help it sink in?"

"It would make my grandmother happy," I said. "So weird that she's a Catholic witch. Two things you just don't think would go together."

"Kind of like you and me. Two things most people wouldn't think go together." He grinned as he grabbed a plate and began to pile food on it. He faced me fully with a mound of food before him. He went to hand it to me.

I snorted. "I cannot eat all of that. No one can."

"There is hardly anything here," he said, trying again to get me to take the plate.

"Uh, Jeffrey, there are four pieces of fried chicken, a mound of mashed sweet potatoes, some sort of green stuff, and whatever that breaded stuff is," I said, pointing to it.

"Breaded okra," he returned.

"I don't even know what that is, let alone how it tastes," I admitted. "What is the green stuff?"

"Collard greens," he said, motioning to corn bread on the counter. "You've got to try that too. Momma's corn bread is to die for."

I couldn't help but laugh at him. Evidently, the way to his heart was through his stomach. Too bad I wouldn't be living up to his mother's cooking skills, unless we were talking about Italian dishes. Then I could probably hold my own.

I took a piece of corn bread and the minute I

tasted it, it melted in my mouth. My eyes widened. It was phenomenal.

I swallowed and stared at him. "I'd have married you for her corn bread alone. Your hot body is just a bonus."

He snorted. "Thanks. I think."

I took another bite and made noises indicating just how yummy it was.

He started to eat as well, standing as he did. "I never asked if you cook."

"Yes, so long as my grandmother isn't in the kitchen," I said. "If she is, I'm not allowed to touch anything without her approval."

"When we get a handle on Dragos, how about we go up and see her?" He drank some of his tea and didn't spit it out.

I cringed for him, remembering the taste of it as I nodded. I took a bite of a piece of fried chicken and flavor exploded in my mouth. "Ohmygod, this is delicious too."

He glanced past me, in the direction of the large picture window that looked out at the water. "Momma will be happy to know you like her food."

"Correction. I *love* it." I ate more, my thoughts going back to our time in the bedroom. "Jeffrey, where did you get your bedroom ceiling fan?"

"Ordered it from the hardware store here in town. Why?" he asked. "If you hate it, I'll change it. As you probably noticed the cabin doesn't have much in the way of a woman's touch."

I glanced around and smiled. "It's perfect as it is. I was wondering about the fan because for a minute I could have sworn it reached jet propulsion levels of air blowing when you we were playing stuff the cannoli."

He watched me carefully. "You felt the gusts of wind too?"

"Uh, *yeah*. They were hard to miss," I replied, taking another bite of the chicken.

"Legs, the night of the succu-witch attack, that storm came out of nowhere," he said, something off in his tone.

"Not really. Sounds like Poppy caused it with her magik," I said, before taking a sip of water.

"Are you sure she did it alone?"

"Marcy may have helped. They're both witch-es," I supplied.

He stared harder at me.

"What?" I asked.

"Legs, you're a witch too," he said softly.

I sat there a second and then realized what he was hinting at. "You think I caused the wind?"

He nodded. "I do."

I snorted, shaking my head. There was *no way* I'd caused the wind.

TWENTY-ONE

Dana

———————

THERE WAS POUNDING on the front door, causing me to jolt slightly on the stool. Jeffrey sniffed the air and set his plate of food down near me on the center island. His eyes widened as he hurried toward the door, throwing it open to reveal Marcy and Poppy standing there.

"What are you doing here?" demanded Jeffrey.

Poppy looked past him, at me.

"Your husband thinks you're at home with Travis watching over you," said Jeffrey sternly as Poppy brushed by him.

"Uh-huh," she said, coming straight for me. "Are you okay?"

"Poppy," said Jeffrey, clearly upset.

I hurried off the stool and met her partway. "I'm fine."

Marcy eased around Jeffrey as if he wasn't even there and came toward me, carrying an oversize bag over her shoulder. I'd seen her take the very same bag to the beach before and wondered what in the world she was up to now. She glanced up at me. "Oh good, you got the ghoul out of your hair. I wasn't sure if you would. I brought a shampoo I made."

Poppy hugged me as Marcy pulled out a dark bottle of liquid. She held it out to Jeffrey, giving him no choice but to take it.

His gaze swept to me for guidance.

I shrugged. When it came to Marcy, it was best to just go with her oddities.

He set the bottle on an end table. "Poppy, where is Travis? Brett said he left him guarding you and the twins."

"Pepper and Tucker went to see Thomas," she said. "Your father actually talked them into it after breakfast this morning. Maria suggested they get him out of town for a bit until this all blows over. They told him they needed to go back to Yale to get their things for summer."

"Did they tell him not to fall for the lure of any

succu-bitches on the way?" I asked, noticing she didn't mention Travis in her response.

Poppy snorted. "It was implied."

Marcy continued digging through her bag. "Poppy, you're going to need to have a long talk with Thomas soon about supernaturals."

"I know, but not today," she said.

Jeffrey touched his brow. "I'll ask this again since you both ignored me. Where is Travis?"

Poppy glanced nervously at me and then pressed a smile to her face. "Um, he's tied up at the moment."

"Doing what?" demanded Jeffrey. "He's supposed to be protecting—"

"Here. Hold this," Marcy said, pulling out a sharpened wooden stake. She thrust it at Jeffrey.

He took the stake, his gaze darting from her to it and then back to her once more. "Why do you have this?"

"Because it was in my bag," she said as if that explained everything.

"Um, Marcy, thank you, but I don't need this. I have built-in weapons," added Jeffrey.

She patted his arm gently. "Aww, you're so adorable. You think I brought that for you. No. It's for Dana."

Jeffrey jerked the stake close to his body. "She's not going up against any threat again. Stake or no stake."

Marcy kept patting his arm. "Sweet that you think so."

Poppy took my hand in hers. "Marcy told me we needed to be here. I know I promised Jeffrey that I'd stay away and let him handle things here with you, but when Marcy told me it was important that we be here—with you—I dropped everything and came."

"You promised Jeffrey you'd stay away from me?" I asked.

She bit her lower lip and nodded. "Earlier. But I hadn't heard from you. I was worried."

He sighed. "I forgot to have her call you. I'm sorry. We were a little busy."

Marcy beamed. "They were knocking boots. Congratulations on mating. I'm so happy for you both."

Poppy squealed and clasped her hands together. "You did it? You let him claim you?"

Jeffrey snorted, setting the stake on the coffee table. "More like demanded."

I groaned. "I did not."

"Did too," he returned with a grin that said he knew darn well he'd baited me.

Poppy yanked me to her and hugged me so tight I thought she might pop my head clean off. I had to push on her to get her to stop. She then jumped up and down in place. "I'm so excited!"

"I couldn't tell," I replied, my tone level.

She squealed again.

Marcy reached into her bag once more. The next I knew, Burgess was darting out of it, running past me and right for the master bedroom.

"You brought your tree-rat in your bag?" I asked.

She nodded. "He was excited to come. He's missed you all day. You should know, I let him sleep in your boot again because he's having a really hard time with you being gone."

I closed my eyes and counted to ten. There was a creepy vampire dude who wanted to harm me, stinky ghouls doing the dude's bidding, and now I had to deal with a squirrel with separation anxiety.

Could my life get any weirder?

There was another pounding on the door, but this one wasn't rapid and light as the last had been. It was strong and loud.

On instinct, I grabbed for my friends and

yanked them behind me as Jeffrey sniffed the air again. His eyes flashed to icy blue and then he grunted, opening the door quickly, his eyes returning to normal.

Brett and Stratton entered.

Jeffrey shut the door. "Oh look, the gang is nearly all here. Should I roll out a welcome mat for anyone else?"

"All here? What do you—" Brett's words died on his lips when he spotted Poppy. He lowered his head slightly, his gaze narrowing on her. "Poppy-seed, *what* are you doing here and where is Travis?"

"We tied him up," said Marcy nonchalantly as she reached into the seemingly bottomless bag. She pulled out a small jar of something. "I made a calming tea for you, Brett."

Stratton laughed. "Did she just say they tied up Travis?"

"She did," returned Brett, annoyance written all over his face.

"She doesn't mean they actually tied him up, does she?" asked Stratton.

"Something tells me that's exactly what she means," interjected Jeffrey. "I think she's going to need a bigger jar of calming tea before the night is out."

Stratton's attention turned to me. He smiled. "Congratulations are in order."

Brett stilled and then looked to his best friend. "You did it? You claimed her?"

Jeffrey licked his lips. "I locked it down. I saw you dance around mating for twenty years. Figured I should just jump in feet first. Sink or swim thing. Well, that and she demanded I do it. Told you chicks dig me."

I shook my head, chuckling as I returned to my plate of food. "Since you're all here, are you hungry? Jeffrey's mom cooked for an army."

Poppy eyed the spread of food on the center island and perked. "She made corn bread? I love her corn bread."

"Right?" I said. "I swear on Richard Marx that it's the best corn bread I've ever had."

"Totally," added Poppy.

Brett yanked out his cell phone and placed a call. He then lowered his phone. "Travis isn't answering."

Marcy held the jar of tea out to him. "Here. You'll need this."

"Did you actually tie him up?" he asked, disbelief on his face.

"Don't be silly," said Marcy, her smile sugary

sweet. "Of course we did."

Brett sounded pained as he bent his head, shaking it as he did.

Poppy went to him and rubbed his upper back as she stood by his side. "There, there, honey. It's okay. We put something in his tea to help him rest. *Then* we tied him up."

"Not helping," he said.

"Travis was supposed to be resting anyway," she countered.

Brett pointed to Marcy. "You are starting to sound like her."

Just then Marcy stilled, her gaze going to the picture window. "*They're* here."

"That wasn't the least bit ominous," added Stratton as he glanced at the window too. "Uh, guys, it's getting very dark out there, very fast."

"Shit," said Jeffrey, rushing to the door and bolting it. He then motioned to me. "Dana, you, Poppy, and Marcy need to go to the master bathroom right this second. Lock yourselves in!"

I didn't panic. Instead, I squared my shoulders. "I can't run and hide, Jeffrey."

"Yes, you can!" he shouted, his eyes flashing to icy blue.

Brett grabbed him. "Reel it in, Farkas."

"I'm not going to let my mate be hurt," snarled Jeffrey.

Poppy glanced at me. "We should have made him a special tea too."

"Let's maybe *not* drug our friends and family," I said.

Marcy glanced at the jar of tea in her hands and then moved it behind her back, doing her best to appear innocent. "Erm, maybe Brett shouldn't have any tea right now then."

Stratton bent as he laughed from the gut.

Brett just looked tired as he kept hold of Jeffrey.

The smell of rotten eggs reached me, and I tensed. "The ghouls are out there."

Stratton straightened and took a moment to regroup. "Right then. Let's do this."

Marcy waved a hand at Brett. "Go stand near the big window. Take Jeffrey with you."

Brett opened his mouth to argue.

Poppy puckered her lips a little and gave him sad eyes.

The man folded in a heartbeat and marched like a scolded child to the position Marcy told him to take. He dragged Jeffrey with him.

"To the left a bit more," she said.

He listened.

Stratton glanced at her. "Where do you want me?"

"Near the back entrance," said Marcy glibly as she opened her bag again. She then yanked out a jug of something that looked like water. She set it on the counter near me.

"How much crap did you put in there?" I asked. "Wasn't it heavy? And how did Burgess make it here without being crushed?"

"I didn't put him on the bottom," she said. "Poppy, get the door."

"Poppy, don't you dare open—"

She was to the door, unbolting it and tossing it open before her mate could finish uttering his protest.

My chest tightened as I locked gazes with a man I'd not seen in twenty years—the same man who had stood outside of the church at my mother's funeral.

My father.

He'd not aged a day.

His black hair hung to his broad shoulders as he filled the door frame. He had to be six foot seven or eight. He made the men currently in the cabin look short and they were all well over six feet tall.

Poppy just stood there, staring up at him.

He glanced down at her and his expression went from unreadable to charming in two point two seconds. "Poppy, nice to formally meet you. I'm Bram Van Helsing."

Gasping, she looked at me, her hand on the open door. "He knows my name?"

I didn't respond.

"Dana, you forgot to mention how attractive he is," she said in a low voice that everyone could still hear.

My jaw set as I stared at Bram.

He sighed. "I never wanted any of this for you, Dana. Please know that. And please know that no matter what you may think of me, I love you very much."

"Well of course you do," said Marcy. "Invite him in, Dana."

I crossed my arms under my breasts and glared at Bram.

Marcy snorted and glanced at Jeffrey. "When you're done with your show of dominance, can you invite him in? If you want to keep your mate safe, he's needed."

"Mate?" asked Bram, his green gaze snapping to Jeffrey.

I found my voice. "If you try to hurt him, I'll use the stake Marcy brought me on you."

Poppy gasped. "Dana!"

The edges of Bram's lips curved upward. "You have a lot of your mother in you. That's a very good thing, Dana."

Jeffrey pushed away from Brett. "Come in."

Bram entered. "My men are nearly here. Jeffrey, it would be wise to summon the pack. I've reached out to the vampires in the territory too. Their master owes me a few favors. They're on their way to assist."

Jeffrey turned his head and stared out the window. He was silent for a moment and when he glanced back at me, his eyes were still icy blue. "It's done. The pack has been alerted."

"Going old school with that summons," said Brett. "Felt that one in my bones."

Bram was just inside the front door when a gust of wind came in out of nowhere, pushing him forward. With a grunt, he regained his footing and stood tall. He rolled his eyes, facing away from the door. "Wilma, I wish I could say it's nice to see you again."

Wilma?

He couldn't possibly be talking about my

grandmother.

In strolled Nonna, her head held high, her purse clutched to her. Behind her came Peter. He had a baseball bat over one shoulder. Next came Rita, carrying a jug of liquid that was oddly similar to the one Marcy had brought. Rita's jug had a symbol on it that looked like a bolt of lightning with a circle drawn through the center.

Then Chester and George entered. They each had golf clubs. Last, but not least, was Lou. He entered pulling his rolling oxygen tank behind him.

"Ohmygod, you really did steal the bus? And you drove here? *This* was your big adventure?" My mouth fell open.

Nonna walked right up to Bram, ignoring my outburst, and threw up a hand gesture meant to ward off evil. A few choice Italian curse words fell from her lips as well.

Bram remained composed. "I see you've warmed to me over the years."

Snapping out of my stunned state, I hurried to Nonna and drew her into a gentle embrace. I then stepped back. "What in the…um…world are you doing here?"

She glared at Bram more before eyeing me. Her gaze raked over me slowly. She frowned.

"Dana, how do you expect to get your mate to notice you if you wear that? It does nothing for your chest. Flattens what little you have."

Poppy snorted.

Marcy rushed in to save me. She eased Nonna away from me. "Good news, her mate noticed her even with her breasts being the size they are."

"He did?" she asked. "Which one is he?"

Marcy pointed to Jeffrey.

Nonna smiled wide and went to him, throwing her arms out.

He glanced at me and then bent to hug her, his eyes going back to normal.

She patted his cheeks and then surveyed him. "We need to fatten you up some. When we're done dealing with the demon and his minions, we'll feed you."

"Okay," said Jeffrey, clearly caught off guard. "It's very nice to meet you, ma'am."

"Call me Nonna," she supplied. "We're family now."

"My condolences," said Bram to Jeffrey.

"Don't push me, vampire," warned Nonna. "Or I'll—"

I stepped in her path to Bram. "Nonna, you

shouldn't be here. Did you notice the darkness outside? That isn't natural. It's not safe for you."

She snorted and rolled her eyes. "That? Please, I've seen darker."

Marcy smiled. "Lou, you should go to the master bedroom and keep watch in there."

He headed in that direction as if he'd been in the house a hundred times before.

She glanced at me. "It's best we tuck him out of harm's way."

Rita giggled. "Lou is always getting underfoot during end-of-the-world moments."

Chester held the end of the golf club and stared around the room. "Whose skull are we smashing?"

I gasped. "Chester?"

He winked at me. "Wouldn't be the first one I took care of."

Nonna nodded to me. "See? I told you I know people."

TWENTY-TWO

Dana

THIS WASN'T HAPPENING. There was no way my ninety-year-old grandmother had boosted a senior center van with her cronies and driven all the way from New York to South Carolina.

I closed my eyes and rubbed them for good measure.

When I opened them, everyone was staring at me like I'd lost my mind.

Rita moved up alongside Nonna and nudged her lightly. "Think she realizes we're not figments of her imagination yet?"

Nonna glanced at Bram. "I'm not sure. He's her father after all."

"Nonna," I said in a hushed breath.

Bram twisted around more and the height

difference between him and Grandma was down-right comical. He made a big production of bending to her level. "You've softened with age."

She curled her lip at him and then hauled off and swatted his shoulder with her clutch bag. "I don't like you."

He feigned shock. "You don't say?"

Marcy eased between them. "Nonna, why don't you come with me into the kitchen area and we can work on some potions? I brought everything we'll need."

Nonna didn't budge from her spot as she continued to give my father the stink eye.

Bram, on the other hand, took a keen interest in Marcy. He didn't so much as blink as he stared at her as she forced Nonna toward the kitchen.

Poppy shook her head. "And here I thought having my dead grandparents haunting the house was the strangest thing I'd see all week."

Rita smiled over at her. "Oh, sweetie, that's just the tip of the iceberg if the cards are right."

Oh goodie. Someone else who was into fortune telling.

The next I knew, Brett was laughing.

Hard.

We all looked at him.

He gave us a knowing stare. "Come on. This is funny. Admit it."

He had a point. It was comical to a certain degree.

Peter headed for the kitchen, bat in hand.

I shook my head at him. "I didn't think you had boosting a bus in you, Peter."

He grinned. "I drove tanks in the Korean War. First ones they equipped us with were crap. They got better ones though. And once I stole one from the enemy. Those were the days."

I simply stared at him, then spoke without a filter. "Don't tanks have driver height requirements?"

He stood up as tall as he could. "I got the job done and didn't take up much room doing it."

I nodded. "Thank you for your service."

He winked and hurried to the kitchen.

Rita followed close behind. "I'll help with the potions. I've always loved making anti-ghoul ones. I brought a base."

"Me too," said Marcy, lifting her hand to high-five Rita.

Much to my surprise, Rita returned the gesture.

Marcy pointed to Rita's jug of liquid. "Nice. I

see you have the symbol for the Slavic goddess of rain and thunder on it."

"Seemed fitting," added Rita with a grin.

Jeffrey growled as he looked out the picture window, the sound low and guttural. "It's darker out there. I smell more of them. What are they waiting for?"

Bram joined him near the window. "I don't know and that's worrisome, *wolf*."

Jeffrey turned his head slowly in Bram's direction, posturing as he did. "Don't take that tone with me."

"Tread carefully," warned Bram. "It would be a shame to have to kill my son-in-law so soon into the relationship."

"You can try, big guy," snarled Jeffrey. "I don't care how old you are. We'll go head-to-head over her. Unlike Kellan, you can't order me away from her."

I gasped. Bram had done that?

He stiffened before glancing at me, appearing nervous.

My hands went to my hips. "Is he right? Did you order Kellan away from me?"

"He was to guard you. Not try to take you to prom," Bram returned, his voice deepening.

I eyed the stake on the table.

Poppy hurried to it and snatched it up, holding it close to her as if she were worried I'd use it to stake Bram. "Let's not kill him more, okay?"

"Do I get a say?" asked Nonna from the kitchen area.

"No," said Marcy and Rita.

Chester and George focused on Jeffrey. "Where do you want us?"

He looked helplessly at me.

Marcy twisted as she pulled more items from her bag. "You could go help Stratton. He's near the back entrance."

Chester narrowed his gaze, determination in his eyes. "On it."

Nodding, George followed.

I was about to comment when the power flickered.

When it cut out, I moved in the direction of Nonna, Rita, and Marcy, worried for their safety.

"Not this way," snapped Nonna. "Take point on the door, Dana."

"What in the hell do you know about taking point?" I asked fast.

"Watch your tone with me, young lady," she warned.

There was a crashing noise from the back of the cabin.

The lights popped on again just as ghouls came busting through the picture window.

Jeffrey, Brett, and Bram reacted quickly.

They each seized a ghoul, stopping them dead in its tracks.

The hair on my neck stood on end as I glanced at the front door.

Poppy was closer to it than me and I knew that was a bad thing. Acting on instinct, I ran at her, sweeping her out of the way gently and turning, taking the brunt of the door as it blew inward.

"Dana!" shouted Jeffrey.

Oddly enough, I wasn't fazed by the strike. All it did was rile my temper. I kicked the door away to find myself standing face-to-face with the ugliest thing I'd ever seen in my life. I couldn't help but recoil.

It sort of resembled a human to some degree. But its skin was grayish and pruned, reminding me a little of a mummy in a museum. Its ears and nose were bat-like. When it lifted a hand, I saw what appeared to be talons.

"Woman, you try my patience," the thing said, making me realize it was Dragos.

I made a gagging noise.

This was the guy who had turned my day on its head?

My temper boiled over. "Good God, have you heard of moisturizer? I'm fairly sure it's been around a while. You should consider soaking in a vat of it because you look like a raisin that was left out in the sun too long."

Dragos hissed.

I waved a hand in front of my face. "Where is Marcy's sage when I need it? Some breath you have there, Dragos. Can you make it dark again? I liked it better when I couldn't see you."

"I will enjoy torturing you," he warned. "When I return you to your father as one of us—a creature of the night, under my control—he will learn his lesson for daring to step into a battle that was not his to join."

I coughed more, the smell of his breath nearly doing me in. "Buddy, seriously, your breath is torture enough."

He snarled and swiped a clawed hand out at me in what suddenly seemed like slow motion. Vaguely, I heard Bram and Jeffrey shouting my name, but my focus was on Dried-Raisin-Dragos. Lifting an arm, I deflected his blow.

"Dana!" yelled Poppy as thunder rumbled outside.

She tossed the stake to me.

Reaching up, I caught it just as Dragos made another move to slash me with his nails. He flashed fangs at me as he did, and I got another whiff of his stale breath. I don't think the man had brushed his teeth once in all his hundreds of years.

I twisted and rammed the stake into his chest. Unlike the vampires I'd dealt with two days prior, he didn't turn into a cloud of ashes.

He laughed sounding downright diabolic. "You missed my heart."

A glance out the front door, as lightning lit the sky, showed me the battle happening there. Austin and other men were fighting ghouls outside.

The distraction cost me as Dragos punched me square in the chest. I went backward and was caught by someone before I'd have hit the floor.

Glancing up, I found Lou standing there, no longer in the room where Marcy had sent him to be out of the way. He nodded to me, righted me and then glanced at Dragos.

Turns out Lou was handier than given credit for during end-of-the-world moments.

The creepster yanked the stake from his chest

and cast it aside. The hole in his chest healed over before my eyes.

Gathering my nerve, I made a move to charge him only to find myself once again being lifted in the air and placed behind Bram. He seemed to make a habit of that during ghoul attacks.

He faced Dragos. "I will be your end."

Dragos laughed wickedly. "You, Vlad, and Harker could not stand against me before. They are not here now. What makes you think you can do so alone?"

I moved out from behind my father and took a stand next to him. "He's not alone."

Dragos watched me carefully. "The daughter I'm told he did not want? The one he never bothered to meet? The one he permitted to grow up with nothing? You would sacrifice yourself for him?"

Bram snarled. "I have always wanted her."

"I can't stand the man and even *I* have to take his side on this," said Nonna from the kitchen, her voice lacking any fear or concern. "He was always lurking, watching her grow up from the shadows. And when he couldn't be there himself, he sent others. And he tried to shower us with gifts and money. My daughter was like me—a proud woman. She'd been hurt when he'd sent her away with a newborn baby."

"I only sent her to you to keep her safe," said Bram. "If I could have, I would've kept my family close to me. I'd have been there for my daughter when she grew up."

"Abraham, it pains me to admit this, but you loved my daughter the best way you knew how," said Nonna. "And seeing as how you managed to father a child with her—someone who wasn't your true mate—that is a testament to just how deep your feelings for her ran. None of this means I like you. I don't."

"Oh I'm well aware of your dislike of me," he said, never taking his eyes from Dragos.

I blinked and in that second, Bram charged Dragos and tackled him through the open front door and out onto the porch. The pair rolled down the steps and onto the walk path.

More thunder and lightning followed.

At the same moment, Jeffrey was knocked out of the already broken window by a group of ghouls. Concern for him filled me, but my gut said that as an alpha male shifter, he'd be fine.

Brett had two ghouls on his back and was

trying to get to Poppy. The sight made me rethink my stance on Jeffrey being able to handle himself.

"Fore!" yelled Chester as he darted into the room, lined up a shot, and took it, striking a ghoul with his golf club. The ghoul's head came off and went right out the open window. What remained of the ghoul fell to the floor.

All I could do was stare at the older man as he wiped ghoul bits off his club like it was just another day on the golf course.

Chester leaned back, glancing down the hall. "That makes three for me, George! What are you up to?"

"What?" yelled George from the back of the cabin.

"I said I killed three!" repeated Chester.

George shouted back, "I can't hear you! Did you say you scored weed for free?"

Lou, who was still in the great room but staying out of the fight, pulled his oxygen mask down some. "He didn't put his ears in."

Chester grumbled. "The man always forgets his hearing aids."

Marcy whistled and held up a vial of something before throwing it at me. I caught it with ease.

"Throw it at the ghouls," she said.

I did. Nothing happened. "That was anti-climactic."

Marcy groaned. "Take the cap off first and *then* throw the liquid at the ghouls."

That made more sense.

She tossed one to Poppy.

Poppy caught the vial of liquid, removed the cap, and lobbed it at a ghoul near her as if the vial was a grenade. Its liquid splashed all over the ghoul.

In the next second, the ghoul popped like a huge zit, drenching Poppy and me in the process.

I looked upward, wiping a bit of it off my chin, thankful it didn't go in my mouth. "Come on! I have ghoul in my hair again!"

Poppy lifted a section of her dark hair. "It's in mine too."

"Ladies," said Brett as he flung a ghoul out the window and snapped another's neck. "Could you please run?"

We ignored him.

Jeffrey leapt through the open window and landed crouched, coming up slowly, looking feral. "Are you hurt?"

I shook my head. "No. Are you?"

His breathing was ragged. "Go to the master

bathroom now! Take the others. Lock yourself in. Hide."

I flicked a piece of ghoul off my shoulder. "*Forgetaboutit.* That's not happening."

Poppy caught another vial of potion from Marcy and then pitched it out the front door, hitting another ghoul with it. She then moved quickly to the side, avoiding more ghoul innards.

"I said go to safety!" shouted Jeffrey. "Can't you women listen?"

Chester pursed his lips and backed out of the room slowly, taking Lou with him. "Come on. You don't want to be here when the women rip him a new one. Peter?"

"Coming," said Peter, hurrying after them. "This is something the young bucks need to learn on their own."

I set my sights on my husband.

So did every other woman in the great room.

Jeffrey froze and then slowly thumbed in the direction of the broken-out window. "I'm going to go back out there and take my chances with the ghouls and a really old vampire. Somehow, I think I stand a better chance out there than in here with y'all right now."

Poppy sighed. "He's smarter than I thought."

"I like him," said Nonna. "I didn't think I would. Shifters are so moody and dramatic. But he's handsome. Dana, how was the cannoli stuffing? Good?"

Brett threw the last of the ghouls out the window and looked toward Jeffrey. He huffed. "How do you like having your bedroom skills questioned by your mate's grandmother? Fun, isn't it?"

"It sucks," said Jeffrey, his gaze on me. "Are you going to answer her? Here is where you sing my praises, Legs."

Lightning struck not far from the cabin, hitting a group of ghouls, drawing my attention.

As another bold of lightning illuminated the sky, I saw Bram and Dragos locked in battle.

My gut said Bram could use help. And while I didn't really know the man, he was blood and I didn't want him dead.

Okay, *more* dead.

"Now would be a good time for the three of you to combine power," said Rita, her gaze on me and then Poppy.

Marcy patted her shoulder gently. "Good thinking. Here, take these."

Rita took a handful of vials. "Have fun."

Marcy came for me and put her hand out. "Trust me, Dana."

I did, so I extended my hand, taking hers in mine.

Poppy hurried to us and took my other hand. As she did, additional thunder and lightning occurred. So did a huge gust of wind. The same gust strength that I'd felt in the bedroom with Jeffrey earlier.

I gasped as I realized he'd been right. I *had* been the cause of it.

"Dana, don't you dare think about—" The sound of a freight train drowned out Jeffrey's voice.

I stared out the open door with my best friends by my side, watching as the darkness diminished enough to see better.

The wind picked up more as did the sound of a locomotive.

Out over the water, I spotted a funnel cloud forming and gasped, nearly letting go of Poppy's hand. Had I caused that too?

She squeezed my hand, holding tight.

The funnel cloud got bigger as it danced on top of the water, coming at the shore rapidly.

"Bram!" I shouted, wanting to warn him since he was in its path.

"He can't hear you," said Marcy loudly.

I tensed and almost closed my eyes to avoid seeing what was going to happen. The strangest urge to yell at Bram again hit me hard and I gave in, except his name didn't fall from my lips. "Dad, behind you!"

Bram's green gaze snapped to me and then he glanced over his shoulder. He seized hold of Dragos and threw him like a rag doll into the air, *at* the funnel cloud, before diving out of the way.

The funnel whipped Dragos higher as a bolt of lightning struck, scoring a direct hit.

My attention went to the discarded stake on the floor, near my foot. In the next moment, it was whipping through the air seemingly on its own, right at Dragos.

This time, it didn't miss.

A plume of ash was the result. Nothing of Dragos remained.

In the blink of an eye, the darkness decreased more, still feeling like night, but no longer pitch black. That was for the best. I wasn't sure how Bram would do in sunlight.

The rest of the ghouls crumbled to the ground, no longer moving. Dark ash rained down from the area Dragos had been.

The funnel cloud dissipated, and the lightning and thunder stopped.

I continued to hold my friends' hands. "D-did we do that?"

"Damn straight we did," said Marcy with attitude. "You don't come at one of us and live to tell the tale. Not when the backup bitches are close."

"Is Dragos dead?" I asked.

"Maybe," said Marcy. "Maybe not. Time will tell."

We released one another, and Poppy ran for Brett.

He swept her up and off her feet, kissing her thoroughly.

I found myself being spun around by Jeffrey.

He cupped my face and then ravished my mouth with his. When he was done, he stared at me and brushed something off my cheek that I strongly suspected used to be part of a ghoul. "Legs, I love you, but we really need to work on you running away from danger, not *at* it."

"Don't waste your breath," said Nonna.

Jeffrey concentrated on me once more. "Maria was right. You *are* a tornado."

My cheeks heated.

"And it is just one more thing I love about you.

What about you, Dana? Is there anything you love about me?"

"Yes." I nodded. There was a lot I loved about him.

"Good." He chuckled. "Now, about my cannoli stuffing skills."

"Dana," said Bram, appearing on the porch.

Jeffrey nudged me slightly. "Legs, give him a chance."

With a small nod, I headed for the porch. When I got there, Bram reached out to touch me but stopped just shy of making contact. He drew his hand back and sighed. "Are you injured?"

"No," I said.

"Good," he returned. "I'll go. Dragos is no longer a threat. My men will handle cleanup here."

The next thing I knew, I was hugging the man. Granted, it was an awkward hug, but a hug all the same.

He wrapped his arms around me, squeezed me tight, and lifted me up off the porch. He then set me down and kissed the top of my head. "I'm sorry for everything. If I had it to do again, I'd change every move I made."

Nodding, I stepped back from him.

"If you're willing, I'd like to have a relationship

with you," he said. "I want to be part of your life and that of your children's lives."

I scoffed. "I'm not really the nurturing type. I don't really see crotch…erm…kids in my future."

Marcy eased up next to me, looping her arm through mine. "Hello, Mr. Dana's Father. Nice to officially meet you. How about we let her be surprised by the news?"

"What news?" I asked.

"Nothing, sugar," she said, wrinkling her nose playfully. "I love you, but you smell like a ghoul —*again*."

Bram stared at Marcy with an odd expression on his face. He didn't blink this time either.

"Are you all right?" I asked.

He cleared his throat, wrenching his gaze from her. "Y-yes."

"That sounded very convincing," I said.

"There you are," said Marcy as Burgess scaled her quickly, taking a seat on her shoulder. She puckered her lips and kissed him. "Good job staying out of harm's way."

Bram's eyes widened. "She just kissed a—"

I shrugged. "You get used to her and him."

Marcy tipped her head as Burgess made tiny noises. She then glanced at Bram. "You don't like squirrels? Like father, like daughter. This is going to be *very* interesting. Bye for now, Mr. Dana's Father."

She went to walk past him, but he stepped in her path. For a second, I wondered if he'd grab her and ravish her. From the look on his face, he was considering it.

"Bram," he said fast. "My name is Bram."

"I know," she said, strolling off toward Austin and the others.

Bram glanced at me. "She's very peculiar."

"Yep," I replied. "She is."

He stared in the direction she'd gone in.

"Bram, what, exactly was Dragos so mad at you about?" I questioned.

He inhaled sharply. "That is a story for another day."

Jeffrey eased up behind me and began rubbing my shoulders. "Legs, why don't you go back to the Proctor House with Brett? You can take your grandmother and her friends there too. This place is a mess right now. I'll get it cleaned up and come and get you."

"Mess?" asked Nonna, something off in her voice. "I don't see a mess."

Jeffrey and I turned to find the window was back to the way it had been prior to the fighting, as was the door. In fact, nothing was out of order. Not to mention, there were no ghoul bodies in the cabin any longer either. It was as if a battle hadn't just occurred.

The only signs there had been one was the fact Poppy was wearing ghoul bits. Her eyes were wide as she stood next to Brett, staring at my grandmother and Rita.

Brett was staring at Nonna too, with a shocked expression on his face.

Stratton and the others were there, but he didn't seem stunned. In fact, he was grinning somewhat.

"W-what in the heck just happened?" asked Jeffrey. "This place was trashed."

"Hmm, strange. It's as if magik came into play," said Nonna, retrieving her clutch and coming toward us. "We'll be at the bed-and-breakfast across town. Enjoy your night, kids."

Brett stopped looking stunned and blinked several times. "I'll head to the Proctor House and check on Travis."

Poppy tugged at her lower lip. "Rogelio has that covered."

"The bird?" asked Jeffrey.

She nodded.

"Grimm Cove is a *very* weird town," I said.

"Totally," added Jeffrey, taking my hand in his. "But you're staying in it, right?"

I nodded.

"Swear it to me," he pressed.

I winked. "I swear it on Richard Marx."

"That'll work, Legs."

THE END

Did you enjoy this book? Want to read Marcy and Bram's story next? Be sure to check out Spell-casting with a Chance of Spirits, book three in the Grimm Cove Series.

Sources

Astarita, Tommaso. *Between Salt Water and Holy Water: a History of Southern Italy*. W.W. Norton, 2006.

Baglio, Matt. *The Rite: The Making of a Modern Exorcist*. Pocket, 2010.

Belanger, M. A. *Dictionary of Demons: Names of the Damned*. Llewellyn, 2020.

"Can You Relocate Without Taking a New Bar Exam?" *Attorney at Work*, 4 Feb. 2020, www.attorneyatwork.com/relocate-ethically-without-taking-new-bar-exam/.

Catholic Answers. "Catafalque." *Catholic Answers*, Catholic Answers, 21 Feb. 2019, www.catholic.com/encyclopedia/catafalque.

Christou, Marios and David Ramenah, directors. *Malin Matsdotter: The Condemned Witch (Occult*

History Explained). Malin Matsdotter: The Condemned Witch (Occult History Explained), The Legends of History, 26 July 2019, youtu.be/WfEess9HC64.

Elworthy, Frederic Thomas. *The Evil Eye an Account of This Ancient & Widespread Superstition: By Frederick Thomas Elworthy With Many Illustrations.* John Murray, Albemarle Street, 1895.

"ExecutedToday.com." *ExecutedToday.com "1676: Malin Matsdotter and Anna Simonsdotter, Ending a Witch Hunt*, 2008, www.executedtoday.com/2008/08/05/1676-malin-matsdotter-and-anna-simonsdotter-ending-a-witch-hunt/.

Florescu, Radu, and Raymond T. McNally. *Dracula, Prince of Many Faces: His Life and His Times.* Back Bay Books, 1990.

"Home Page." *New York Foundation for Senior Citizens*, 2020, www.nyfsc.org/.

Illes, Judika. *Encyclopedia of Spirits: The Ultimate Guide to the Magic of Fairies, Genies, Demons, Ghosts, Gods & Goddesses.* HarperCollins e-Books, 2010.

Knowles, Larry. *Korean War Letters from a Lieutenant and His Bride.* Dorrance Publishing Co., Inc., 2011.

Kryuchkova, Olga. *Creation of Protective Talismans Using Ancient Slavic Symbols. Apotropaic Magic.* Babelcube INC, 2020.

Künecke, Janina, et al. "Facial Responsiveness of Psychopaths to the Emotional Expressions of Others." *PloS One*, Public Library of Science, 11 Jan. 2018, www.ncbi.nlm.nih.gov/pmc/articles/PMC5764293/.

Lester, Paul B [VNV], et al. *Leadership in Dangerous Situations: a Handbook for the Armed Forces, Emergency Services, and First Responders.* Naval Institute Press, 2011.

Mack, Carol K. *Field Guide to Demons, Fairies, Fallen Angels, and Other Subversive Spirits.* W W Norton, 2011.

"Main Menu." *On Balance Search*, 24 Feb. 2016, www.onbalancesearch.com/blog-page/reciprocity-what-states-can-you-practice-law/.

McNally, Raymond. *In Search of Dracula: The History of Dracula and Vampires.* Houghton Mifflin., 1994.

Riquelme, John Paul., and Bram Stoker. *Dracula, Bram Stoker: Complete, Authoritative Text with Biographical, Historical, and Cultural Contexts, Critical History, and Essays from Contemporary Critical Perspectives.* Bedford/St. Martins, 2002.

Sides, Hampton. *On Desperate Ground: The Marines at the Reservoir, the Korean War's Greatest Battle.* Anchor Books, 2019.

Skal, David J. *Something in the Blood: The Untold Story of Bram Stoker, the Man Who Wrote Dracula.* Liveright Publishing Corporation, 2017.

Sosbrooklyn. "Manhattan District Attorney's Office." *Manhattan District Attorney's Office*, 9 Apr. 2020, www.manhattanda.org/.

"South Carolina Bar." *South Carolina Bar*, 2020, www.scbar.org/.

Staff, Bio. "Bewitched: 5 Real Witches in History." *Biography.com*, A&E Networks Television, 31 Oct. 2019, www.biography.com/news/real-witches-in-history.

"Yale University Virtual Tour." *Yale College Undergraduate Admissions*, 2020, admissions.yale.edu/virtual-tour.

About the Author

Dear Reader

Did you enjoy this title and want to know more about Mandy M. Roth, her pen names and all the titles she has available for purchase (over 100)?

About Mandy:

New York Times & *USA TODAY* Bestselling Author Mandy M. Roth loves 80s music and movies and wishes leg warmers would come back into fashion. She also thinks the movie The Breakfast Club should be mandatory viewing for...okay, everyone. When she's not dancing around her office to the sounds of the 80s or writing books, she can be found designing book covers for New York publishers, small presses, and indie authors.

CPSIA information can be obtained
at www.ICGtesting.com
Printed in the USA
LVHW010518210720
661148LV00006B/1155